FOR FEAR OF]

JOHN BLACKBURN was born in 1923 in
the second son of a clergyman. Black¹
near London beginning in 1937, but ~~~~~~~~ ~~~ ~~~~~~~~~ ~~
the onset of World War II; the shadow of the war, and that of Nazi
Germany, would later play a role in many of his works. He served as a
radio officer during the war in the Mercantile Marine from 1942 to 1945,
and resumed his education afterwards at Durham University, earning his
bachelor's degree in 1949. Blackburn taught for several years after that,
first in London and then in Berlin, and married Joan Mary Clift in 1950.
Returning to London in 1952, he took over the management of Red Lion
Books.

It was there that Blackburn began writing, and the immediate success in 1958 of his first novel, *A Scent of New-Mown Hay*, led him to take
up a career as a writer full time. He and his wife also maintained an
antiquarian bookstore, a secondary career that would inform some of
Blackburn's work, including the bibliomystery *Blue Octavo* (1963). *A Scent
of New-Mown Hay* typified the approach that would come to character-
ize Blackburn's twenty-eight novels, which defied easy categorization in
their unique and compelling mixture of the genres of science fiction,
horror, mystery, and thriller. Many of Blackburn's best novels came in
the late 1960s and early 1970s, with a string of successes that included the
classics *A Ring of Roses* (1965), *Children of the Night* (1966), *Nothing but the
Night* (1968; adapted for a 1973 film starring Christopher Lee and Peter
Cushing), *Devil Daddy* (1972) and *Our Lady of Pain* (1974). Somewhat un-
usually for a popular horror writer, Blackburn's novels were not only successful with the reading public but also won widespread critical acclaim:
the *Times Literary Supplement* declared him 'today's master of horror' and
compared him with the Grimm Brothers, while the *Penguin Encyclopedia
of Horror and the Supernatural* regarded him as 'certainly the best British
novelist in his field' and the *St James Guide to Crime & Mystery Writers*
called him 'one of England's best practicing novelists in the tradition of
the thriller novel'.

By the time Blackburn published his final novel in 1985, much of his
work was already out of print, an inexplicable neglect that continued
until Valancourt began republishing his novels in 2013. John Blackburn
died in 1993.

By John Blackburn

A Scent of New-Mown Hay (1958)★
A Sour Apple Tree (1958)
Broken Boy (1959)★
Dead Man Running (1960)
The Gaunt Woman (1962)
Blue Octavo (1963)★
Colonel Bogus (1964)
The Winds of Midnight (1964)
A Ring of Roses (1965)★
Children of the Night (1966)★
The Flame and the Wind (1967)★
Nothing but the Night (1968)★
The Young Man from Lima (1968)
Bury Him Darkly (1969)★
Blow the House Down (1970)★
The Household Traitors (1971)★
Devil Daddy (1972)★
For Fear of Little Men (1972)★
Deep Among the Dead Men (1973)
Our Lady of Pain (1974)★
Mister Brown's Bodies (1975)
The Face of the Lion (1976)★
The Cyclops Goblet (1977)★
Dead Man's Handle (1978)
The Sins of the Father (1979)
A Beastly Business (1982)★
A Book of the Dead (1984)★
The Bad Penny (1985)★

★ Available from Valancourt Books

FOR FEAR OF LITTLE MEN

JOHN BLACKBURN

VALANCOURT BOOKS

For Fear of Little Men by John Blackburn
First published London: Jonathan Cape, 1972
First Valancourt Books edition 2022

Published by Valancourt Books, Richmond, Virginia
http://www.valancourtbooks.com

ISBN 978-1-954321-68-7 (*trade paperback*)
ISBN 978-1-954321-71-7 (*trade hardcover*)
Also available as an electronic book.

Set in Dante MT
Cover by Matthew Revert

Up the airy mountain
Down the rushy glen.
We daren't go a-hunting
For fear of little men.

Prologue

What was wrong with him? What had he wanted from her? Why had he given her good money for nothing? Miss Ameera O'Brien stared at the notes tucked away in her dressing-table drawer. Why should anyone pay twenty pounds to spend the night with a prostitute and then take sleeping-pills?

What was going on in his mind? Ameera closed the drawer and glanced at the bed. The man lay on his back with his hands clenched together, and though he was snoring loudly he was comparatively quiet now. The snores were nothing to what had gone before. For much of the night he had kept grinding his teeth till she thought they would be torn from the gums, at times he had screamed and whimpered in his sleep, and for hours on end a chanting, sobbing sound had burbled from his lips.

What could cause such misery? Ameera was a half-caste, she had followed her profession for over half of her twenty-nine years and practised it across half the world. She had imagined that no idiosyncrasy of the human male would ever surprise her, but she realized she was wrong. She'd had to entertain some odd clients in her time, but never one like this.

The strange thing was that he'd appeared perfectly normal till they had undressed and she tried to put her arms around him. Then he'd drawn back and shaken his head, and for a moment she imagined that his trouble was impotence. That he had hoped to find confidence with a stranger, and known that failure was inevitable. But she was wrong, because the pattern was different and those poor devils always acted in the same way. An initial, hopeful and sometimes violent attempt, a second not so violent; finally the despairing third, followed by an acceptance that anxiety remained stronger than lust and defeat was ordained. After that came the talk. They always wanted to talk and blame their inadequacies on frigid wives, war wounds, unhappy childhoods or drink. Usually drink: 'Sorry, sweetie, had a skinful, but next time I'll be sober and then . . . Wow.'

This man had been quite sober, he'd made no attempt at all and spoken very little. He'd swallowed his pills and edged away when she joined him on the bed. 'You are an attractive woman, Miss O'Brien,' he had said, 'and please don't be offended by my ungallantry. I am very tired, sleep is all I want, but I would like you to stay close beside me till the morning. If I try to get out of bed, please wake me immediately. Will you do that, my dear?

'Thank you.' He had smiled gratefully when she agreed. 'I hope I will not disturb you, because I suffer from rather a tiresome dream.'

Miss O'Brien, indeed! Ameera had been slightly offended by his formality and lack of interest, but she was tired herself and welcomed the prospect of a good night's rest. Twenty quid for seven-eighths of nine-tenths of F— all, she had thought when she turned out the light. But there was no rest for her; a few minutes later the noises had begun and they continued till dawn. The snores, the screams and whimpers, the teeth grinding and the sobbing, chantlike sound that made her think of a mob rampaging in the distance. Nobody could have slept with such a bedfellow, and even if she'd been stone-deaf the tension that flowed from his body like an electric current would have kept her awake.

He'd come prepared to spend the night away from home, which was another odd thing. It was morning at last, the sun was rising over London and through a chink in the curtain a ray of light fell on the wash-basin and the equipment her visitor had brought with him. A toothbrush, toothpaste, a portable electric razor and the bottle of purple-blue capsules which Ameera recognized as 'blue jays': sodium amytal. Two of them had put him out, but they had certainly not given him peace of mind.

'God! Was that it? Could he be in trouble with the law?' Ameera's face became tense and she tiptoed across the little, cosy room. The man's suit lay folded on a chair by the window, and though it looked eminently respectable, appearances meant nothing and she felt very anxious as she reached into the breast-pocket. Was he on the run, perhaps? A wanted criminal desperate for a place to sleep, who needed her bed because the hotels and boarding-houses had his description? Were dreams of capture and imprisonment torturing him? If so, she'd call Chundra and have him thrown out and quick about it. Ameera and her protector, Chundra Ghosh, were illegal immigrants and they wanted no dealings with the police.

Wrong again, thank goodness. She replaced the wallet with a relieved smile. Hunted criminals do not parade their identities with driving licences and cheque-books and credit cards. Men on the run rarely live in the stockbroker belt or belong to exclusive clubs.

So, just what was the matter with him and why had he picked her up? She pulled back the curtain to let the sunlight fall on the face on the pillow, and quite suddenly a portion of the truth became clear to her. The man had paid twenty pounds to sleep with her because he was too frightened to sleep alone.

'Where ... what ... who are you?' The light had awakened him, the snores had stopped and his eyes were open. 'Of course. Yes, I remember.' He looked at his watch on the bed-side table. 'Good morning, Miss O'Brien. I hope I didn't give you a restless night.'

'Not a pleasant one.' Now that she knew he was not a criminal Ameera looked at her visitor more sympathetically. He was tallish and middle-aged, and his manner had been formal and slightly pedantic when he approached her in the

Frith Street club. He had inquired what her terms were and accepted them as though they were making some routine business arrangement; imagining that he might be a professional man, perhaps a doctor or a lawyer, she had been rather flattered by his attentions. Now the once-firm features were sagging, the eyes were bloodshot and the stubble on his jaw was damp with sweat and saliva. He made her think of a patient regaining consciousness after a serious operation.

'We've both had one hell of a night, and I've been worried about you.' Ameera took a packet of cigarettes from her dressing-gown pocket and lit one herself when he refused. 'Do you have a lot of bad nightmares?'

'Not a lot . . . only one, in fact.' He eased himself out of bed and groped forward towards the wash-basin. The effects of the pills and his troubled sleep were still with him and Ameera laid a steadying hand on his arm.

'Thank you . . . thank you very much. You're a kind woman, Miss O'Brien.' She had turned on the taps and he bent down and sluiced his face.

'Yes, one solitary dream is my problem.' He straightened from the basin. The water had done a lot to revive him, his features had lost their puffiness, but his eyes were still stricken. 'I suffer from one nightmare that has been recurring at regular intervals during the last two years and never varies in a single detail.'

'A dream that is always the same. How horrible.' Ameera handed him a towel. 'And it frightens you so badly that you daren't sleep by yourself?'

'Quite true, my dear.' He picked up the razor and started to remove his stubble. 'However, other people's dreams are boring subjects and I won't inflict mine on you.'

'But I'm interested in dreams and I'd like to hear about yours.' Her father had been the drunken second mate of a freighter plying between Liverpool and Calcutta, but on her mother's side Ameera came from a long line of pimps and harlots and brothel-keepers and she took her career very seriously indeed. She regarded herself as a professional woman, providing her services in much the same way as a doctor or a dentist. She did her utmost to satisfy her clients, and believed that sympathy and the receipt of confidences were sometimes as important as physical gratification. This man had not quibbled at her price, he was in extreme mental distress and she felt duty-bound to help him if she could. Also, as she had said, she was very interested in dreams. 'Please tell me what you experience in your dream. Talking about these things can help, you know.'

'If you really mean it.' He had cleaned his teeth and walked over to his clothes on the chair. His steps were quite firm now and his voice as pedantic as when he had first spoken to her in the club. 'But do stop me if I distress you, Miss O'Brien. Some of the details are far from pleasant.' He buttoned up his shirt, pulled on the trousers of his well-pressed suit and began to talk.

'You're quite right, that is horrible.' He had finished at last, and Ameera shivered slightly because the story had shocked her deeply.

'And you've been having that same dream for over two years and it never alters at all. Yes, I can understand why you want to have somebody near you at night. If you were on your own you might go round the bend and try to kill yourself. But what are you doing about it? Surely you've seen a doctor?'

'Several doctors, my dear. I may be going round the bend, as you say, but I'm not a complete fool.' He was adjusting his tie before a mirror and Ameera saw his lips curl cynically. 'Two general practitioners, a neurologist and a psychiatrist have studied my case and I have been treated with drugs, psychoanalysis and put on various health-giving diets. I have also consulted a faith-healer, and a clergyman who advised me to marry and take up golf or devote my leisure to charitable activities.

'As you yourself know, the suggestion of marriage is hardly practicable. I am not a very restful sleeping-partner.' He spoke with only a slight trace of bitterness as though discussing some tiresome domestic problem: a wife's extravagance, a son's school report, a daughter's unsuitable boy-friend. 'With one exception my advisers assured me that the phenomenon must have a purely rational cause and they all promised that it would pass in time. The last promise was made six months ago and I don't have to tell you how reliable it was.'

'Not one of them could help you?' Ameera's curiosity was rising rapidly, because Chundra Ghosh had often talked about cases like this. People might jeer at Chundra's fortune-telling and mind-reading and dismiss them as conjuring tricks, and she knew that he was nine-tenths charlatan; he'd openly admitted it to her. But she also knew that a tenth of the power he claimed was quite genuine, and he'd told her things about herself to prove it. 'The dream takes place about once a week and doesn't vary in any way?'

'Not in the smallest detail, Miss O'Brien.' The man combed his hair and frowned at his face in the glass. You're going mad, he thought, looking at the reflection of Ameera's room and considering his other hiding-places. Harlots' beds, Turkish baths, late-night cinemas, anywhere for company. But one day there'll be no refuge, you'll be quite alone and you'll be driven crazy, gaga, out of your mind. Then they'll take you away, lock you up by yourself, and that'll be the end of you.

'In fact, the experience becomes stronger and more vivid as time progresses, and recently there has been another phenomenon which I think of as a safety-valve. During the last few months I have been warned when the dream is due to take place. Aircraft warn me.

'It's perfectly true, my dear. That is why I keep myself prepared.' He started to gather up his toilet things: the toothpaste and brush, the razor and the sleeping-pills. 'Take last night, for example. I had to work late, and I was walking to the station when an airliner, an FP 178, flew overhead. As I listened to the exhaust note it suddenly changed and became a voice. A voice speaking in some foreign language I couldn't understand, but I sensed the gist of what was being said. The voice was a warning . . . It was warning me that as soon as I closed my eyes I would start to dream. That's why I went to Soho to find company.

'And I'm very grateful to you for your company, my dear.' He picked up his hat and bowed. 'Goodbye, and please accept my apologies for spoiling your beauty sleep.'

'No, don't go. You must tell me more.' He had turned to the door, but Ameera gripped his wrist. She had to know more, because curiosity had turned to excitement. Europeans always tried to explain such matters in material terms, but her mother's people knew better. A dream that gave warning of its approach and was constantly repeated over the years could mean that one of the forbidden doors was ajar. An unlikely thing to have happened to an unbeliever, a prosaic, middle-class Englishman, but if it had, there might be ways to open the door still further.

'You said that the doctors and the priest told you that the dream must have a rational cause?' She studied his face before asking the question. A good face apart from the troubled eyes. Firm-featured, and strong, but not a face that showed much personality or imagination. The face of a man who can acquire knowledge, but does not create. 'What did the faith-healer tell you?'

'Something quite nonsensical, though a woman of your race might just believe it, Miss O'Brien.' He stressed the Irish name mockingly. 'The faith-healer suggested that I might be reliving something that had actually happened . . . experiencing an event that took place in a former life.

'But there is scant evidence for reincarnation, thank God, though naturally I considered the possibility. I've considered a hundred possibilities, if it comes to that.' He shrugged and shook his head. 'To take any such notion seriously I would have to prove that what I witness in my dream was an actual historical event. I would then have to find the location of that event and see if my images tally with reality. To be at all certain, I would somehow have to discover people who both figure in my dream and also share it. As I told you, I see a great number of them and their faces are completely clear to me. If I find just one of them, and he or she shares my experiences and suffers as I do . . .' He shrugged again. 'Rather difficult tasks, I'm afraid.'

'But not impossible, perhaps.' Ameera's excitement was really on the boil, because she had just remembered something Chundra had told her. A child . . . a nine-year-old boy from Madras had also had a recurrent dream in which he was a member of a crowd that was trapped in a city square and being fired upon by soldiers. His descriptions were so vivid that the newspapers reported the story, and some time later a woman in Bombay claimed that she had the same experience. She and the boy were brought together, they recognized each other instantly and, after certain treatment was given them, they spoke their dreams aloud. Historical records showed that both were reliving the Amritsar massacre which took place eighteen years before the woman was born.

'Listen,' Ameera said. 'Nobody has been able to help you so far, but I have a friend who might. He is only young and people laugh at him, but I know that he has certain powers, because he has demonstrated them to me. If you are experiencing something from the past, he might be able to lead you back through time and show you what it was and who you were. Once that happened – once you knew the truth, the dream might stop troubling you. So please let my friend try. Please talk to Chundra, sir. You said you were being driven mad, and even if he can't help you, you have nothing to lose.'

'That is true enough.' The man glanced at his watch with a smile. He prided himself on a sense of humour, it was still early and he certainly had nothing to lose. The experts had failed, so why not let Ameera's ponce have a go? He had time to kill, and some Hindu conjuror dabbling in magic could do no harm. He would do no good either, but anything was worth a try and the performance might be amusing.

'Lead me to your wizard, Miss O'Brien,' he said, still smiling as Ameera hurried to the door.

* * *

'Do not move a muscle, sahib. Look at the ink in your hands and concentrate hard. Keep your eyes fixed on the ink pools and they will become mirrors of the past. That is all you have to do, and we shall go back together. Right back to the source – the place where it all began.' Chundra Ghosh was a fat, full-blooded Bengali in his twenties. He wore a white turban, a green dressing-gown over red-and-white pyjamas, and his leather bedroom-slippers had scarlet buckles. He looked as sleek as a performing sea-lion and just about as impressive, and his room was in keeping with his appearance; the walls decorated with travel posters and pin-ups cut from magazines, and the bookcase filled with brightly jacketed science-fiction novels. The only eastern influences were the turban and a brass statuette of Vishnu, the god of preservation.

'No drugs have been administered, there will be no hypnosis, but you must not move your eyes. It is the ink that will move – if you concentrate on it and keep tense, sahib. Give me tension and Vishnu will roll time into reverse and reveal the things that trouble you.' He eyed Ameera's client sternly, sensing cynicism beneath the obedient expression. The man sat facing the god's image, with his hands stretched out on a table. A dark, liquid blotch lay in each of his palms, and between them camphor pellets spluttered on a spirit stove.

'Be tense, very tense, sahib, and if a door is ajar we shall open it. In the past you have only experienced these things

while you slept, but now they are going to appear in the sunlight and with your eyes open.' Mr Ghosh stared down at the
ink pools in the man's hands and sniffed the camphor. 'Keep
looking at the ink, breathe in deeply while you talk, and repeat
exactly how the dream first came to you.'

'I was at London Airport waiting for a friend whose flight
was late, and I went up to the public enclosure and watched
the planes landing and taking off. I closed my eyes for a
moment and listened to the different exhaust notes. I am connected with the industry, you see, and the problem of aircraft
noise has always concerned me.' What a fool you are, the man
told himself while he talked. How can a ponce and a half-caste
street-walker help you? The supernatural does not exist and
you are mentally ill. Get up from the table, wash your hands,
give them another fiver for their trouble and go home.

His eyes flickered, he tried to raise his head, but all at
once he found that he couldn't, because the ink really was in
motion and pictures were forming on its surface. Ameera's
face and seven other faces were floating in the liquid and they
were dark and fair, young and raddled, friendly and bitter
and bored. The faces of women whose beds he had shared
because he dreaded meeting the dream alone.

'There was a lot of traffic moving, Mr Ghosh. Jets and
turbo-props and an old piston-engined aircraft revving up.
And quite suddenly while I listened to them they all seemed to
join together and become a chant, a great choir singing to me
in some language I felt I should understand. I must have dozed
off then, but just before I fell asleep I realized that I had to . . .
had to . . . must relearn . . .' He broke off because the ink was
moving violently now. It was boiling, and other images were
appearing, rising up to him from the frothing liquid. The camphor smell had changed into the reek of high-octane petrol,
the room had become the airport enclosure and the dream
was beginning. Soon he would see and hear them again with
his eyes wide open in the sunlight. Those posturing bodies of

the conquerors, the chant, the thud as they broke the poor dying body. Soon every face would be clear to him except the face of one man. The only one who mattered. The tortured one whose back was turned towards him, his blond hair flowing in the breeze and his muscles knotted against the ropes that held him. The god, daemon, master, who had to be freed, and he felt cords bite into his own flesh as he fought to break loose and go to the rescue.

'Ullah . . . ullah . . . ullah.' What was happening . . . why had the dream changed? And surely that was his own voice singing? Why was everything different? On each other occasion he had been given a vision of death and despair, but all at once he felt hope because he realized what the chant meant. He realized that defeat was not inevitable, because his god could not die. The body might rot, but the spirit survive.

'Stay where you are, sahib.' The sound of an aircraft flying low over the rooftops came through the half-open window and Chundra Ghosh raised his voice. 'It is coming back, but you must not move. You must keep on concentrating and we will unearth the truth together.'

'But I know the truth.' The table toppled forward and the man stood upright with the ink dribbling from his hands. The pictures and the sounds had faded and he was back in the Soho room with Ameera and Mr Ghosh. Everything was quite normal again, except Mr Ghosh. Mr Ghosh was growing bigger.

'You want me to return, don't you,' the man said, knowing what his god was and watching the green dressing-gown split open like the skin of a cocoon. Mr Ghosh's body had burst through the cloth, his turban was rising to the ceiling, his dark face was becoming fair.

'It's too late – too long ago. You're dead and I am a man – a man – a man. I can't go back to you. I don't even know where you are.' He cowered away as Mr Ghosh came towards him, his turban scraping the ceiling though his knees were on the floor. Mr Ghosh was gigantic, but he was also deformed. His legs hinged unnaturally and he was crawling on broken joints.

'Ullah . . . ullah . . . ullah,' sobbed the aircraft in the distance.

'Control yourself, sahib. No cause for alarm,' said Mr Ghosh, holding out a restraining hand.

'I want you back . . . I want all of you back,' said the thing, crawling along the floor.

'No,' said the man.

'Please, sahib,' said Mr Ghosh.

'For the love of God,' said Ameera O'Brien as she ran forward. But she was too late. Before she or Chundra Ghosh could reach him, her guest had turned, opened the window wide and thrown himself out.

Chapter One

'Pollution? Of course pollution must have been responsible, Charles. That word has become pretty all-embracing lately.' Sir Marcus Levin, K.C.B., F.R.S., and recent winner of a Nobel Prize for services to medicine, looked with professional detachment at the evidence of death lying on the desk before him. Empty lobster shells, diseased gulls flopping listlessly on an island, a beach littered with rotting fish.

'You say that they haven't isolated the substance responsible, but there could be a dozen sources.' He turned to two aerial photographs of the Linsleat estuary in Northern Ireland. One was four years out of date and showed a desolate stretch of water with a few farms dotted around the surrounding hills, a fishing village near the mouth and an island white with seabirds. The second was present-day, and it proved what mankind could do. Steam plumed from the nuclear power station, factories and houses and caravan sites sprawled along the banks of the river, and concrete buildings of a new town faced the Atlantic like the tents of an encamped army. Only the island, which had been preserved as a bird sanctuary, was left to nature.

'But why the concern, Charles? What do a few animals matter when we have the march of progress to consider? There is a population explosion . . . Belfast's housing problem had to be solved, so let the weakest go to the wall as usual.'

Sir Marcus spoke cynically, but the phrase 'housing problem' brought a series of images to his mind. Huts, compounds and railway trucks, and all of them had been overcrowded, tightly packed with men and women who were very close to death. Marcus Levin was an eminent and successful man at the height of his career, and he looked it. He had a young wife whom he adored, he had his title and his fellowship and his Nobel Prize, and since his isolation of the Enterin 165 virus he had been regarded as one of the world's foremost bacteriologists. But he also had a chip like a slab of concrete slung to his shoulders, because though he had come a long way, most of it had been a road through hell. He had endured the battle of the Warsaw ghetto, the Ruhr labour camps and Belsen. He had slaved all day in a London factory, attended classes every evening, and each night he had knelt down and prayed that a British medical school would one day accept him. After that had come the long, desperate struggle for his degree and the fellowships won against men with ten times his advantages. That was in the past, he had tried to shrug aside bitterness, but not very long ago he had lost something he craved for and the wounds had reopened. Beneath the beautifully cut suit that had cost him a hundred and fifty guineas, the well-groomed hair which was still without a trace of grey and the studied professional manner of wisdom and confidence, the memories festered.

'But what else did they expect, Charles?' he said, picking up a Ministry report. 'Sewage from the new town, discharge from the power station, factories pouring out industrial effluent. There was bound to be trouble and the only interesting thing is how some of the poor little blighters managed to survive and adjust themselves to their new environment.

'Yes, survival is fascinating.' Marcus had always been awed by the tenacity of nature; he was a survivor himself, and quite out of the blue the 'super' rats that were ravaging Shropshire crossed his mind. Their infestation might be a blow to farmers, but it was a very wonderful thing. Larger, stronger, more voracious rats – not only had they developed immunity to Warfarin, the poison that had once ravaged them; they enjoyed eating it, they sought it out, they thrived on it.

The first warnings had come to Linsleat in May. Despite development, the estuary still supported a profitable fishing industry: Linsleat lobsters and oysters were highly prized, and anglers flocked to the river during the salmon season. But this year the salmon did not run. As if sensing danger, they kept away and found fresh breeding grounds. Other fish were scarce too, and after a gale shoals of dead herring and mackerel were washed ashore. Soon after that, the warden of the bird sanctuary reported trouble. His charges had laid plentifully, the eggs hatched normally and the chicks appeared healthy. But as they matured, the young birds became debilitated. Some were stunted, others never developed the ability to fly or swim, and within a few weeks the island stank of corruption.

Next to suffer were the shellfish. Though the oyster-beds were unaffected and gave a plentiful yield, lobsters were scarce and the few specimens were either old or undersized. When skin-divers were sent down, they found that the seabed was littered with empty shells and rotting corpses.

But the extraordinary thing was survival. Sir Marcus considered the individuals that had escaped. As had happened with wildlife after the early atomic tests in the Pacific, they appeared to have undergone glandular changes which allowed them to deal with their hostile environment. However these defence mechanisms were produced, they had proved effective and once again fish swarmed in the water and birds wheeled over the island. Extremely interesting, he thought. Very wonderful indeed, but hardly his business. After all, he was a bacteriologist; he dealt with animate destroyers of life, and the Linsleat outbreak seemed to have been caused by chemical or nuclear contamination.

'Like several other experts, you agree that pollution must be to blame, Mark.' General Charles Kirk of Foreign Office Intelligence had just lit a cigar with proper ceremony. He was an old, heavily built man with a scarred hand, a thick grey moustache and a passion for heat. A tweed suit and a cardigan increased his bulk, and though it was a warm day, an electric fire glowed before his desk.

'Yes, it would seem quite clear that those fish and birds were the victims of pollution, but apparently that is not the case. Not according to these statements, anyway.' Kirk's left hand, which lacked three fingers, rapped a pile of papers.

'Analysis shows that the water is now perfectly pure, and every possible source appears to be above reproach.' Kirk considered the statements he had been reading. From the Electricity Board denying the possibility of any atomic leakage from their power station. From the borough engineer of Linsleat New Town testifying to the excellence of his sewage disposal plant. From factory managers and hoteliers and owners of caravan and chalet sites. From the Admiralty confirming that since a Norwegian tanker was prosecuted for oil dumping two years ago there had been no further cases in the area. Everybody claimed to be innocent and the only witnesses against them were dead fish and sea-birds.

'Toxic waste must have been discharged, and there's bound to be a source, though obviously it's dried up now.' Marcus eased his chair away from the desk. He was very fond of Kirk, but his friend's passion for warmth could be very trying. The office windows were tightly closed and the atmosphere was as hot as a Kew glass-house. 'Somebody must have been reckless or criminally negligent, but I'm interested to know why water pollution should concern you, Charles. I thought your job was security – catching spies and so forth.'

'Security is my job, old boy, and I don't have to tell you how tricky the situation in Northern Ireland still is, or that the Linsleat development has been a bone of contention from the word go. Catholics complain that all the plum jobs went to the Protestants. Protestants feel that the housing facilities have been unfairly divided. At any moment Linsleat may turn into a second Londonderry, and this pollution could spark off violence unless we can expose the culprits.

'I'm not exaggerating, Mark, because the witch hunters are hard at work.' He handed over a selection of Photostats. 'These are letters written to the Irish newspapers and they'll show you what the mood is.'

'Good grief.' Mark shook his head in near disbelief. Most of the letters were too libellous for publication and were written by cranks. A Nonconformist minister considered that the estuary had been deliberately polluted by I.R.A. terrorists. A Catholic schoolmaster hotly denied any I.R.A. involvement but agreed that poison had been deliberately introduced; in his opinion the malefactors were Russian trawlers who often fished off Linsleat and their aim was the destruction of Ireland's natural resources. Another Catholic claimed that the power station was to blame; its reactors were of an experimental type which was unreliable and should never have been installed, and there was grave danger to human life. A man called James Doonen, who signed himself 'Ulster Forever', was also worried about the power station and feared that Catholic workmen employed there were planning sabotage.

'Yes, they're all lunatics, and at the moment there is nothing to worry about.' Kirk pulled at his cigar and stared at the grey smoke drifting up to the ceiling. 'But in times of trouble people listen to loonies, and if there was another epidemic at Linsleat, if human life was affected, things might become unpleasant.

'So, I want to find where the poison came from, Mark, and that's why I need your help. You see, with one exception, the establishments which might be responsible are perfectly prepared to open their premises and plant for independent inspection. But these jokers won't, and there's no pressure we can put on them. The powers-that-be won't make them open up for the sake of a few fish and sea-birds.' Mark had laid down the letters, and Kirk passed over two photographs. One showed a factory building with D.R. PRODUCTS inscribed in huge letters over the entrance; the other, a man's face. 'D.R. Products have refused to co-operate and state categorically that any effluent they discharge is harmless to life. As their premises were inspected by the Ministry of Health last January and given clearance, there's not a damn thing we can do about it.'

'That's rather suspicious.' Mark looked at the second photograph. 'Refusal makes them an obvious choice of culprit.'

'Quite so. Either they've got something to hide or Herr Doktor Graebe, the fellow you're looking at, is merely pig-headed. An arrogant kraut who likes to stand on his rights.'

'Graebe – his full name's Hans Graebe, isn't it?' Mark was still studying the picture. 'He rings a bell, but I can't place him, Charles.'

'You should be able to, old boy. After all, you're a Jew who only escaped the gas chambers by a miracle.' The general massaged his torn hand before the fire. 'Graebe is a chemist, a very brilliant one, and during the war he did research work on nerve gases; at least, that's the official story. In '46 he was tried by an Allied tribunal for crimes against humanity and acquitted. Legally the verdict was correct – there was no evidence against him – but in my opinion he was as guilty as hell.' Kirk's usually urbane voice had a savage ring. 'I sat through some of the hearing, Mark; I could sense his guilt across the courtroom, and I'm damned sure that the bastard should have been strung up before he could say "Heil Hitler!"

'However, he got away with it and last year he came to this country after being appointed chief chemist and general manager of D.R. Products' Linsleat plant. D.R. produces synthetic resins, they have a lot of waste to get rid of, but I don't side with our letter-writing friends about deliberate pollution. I can't swallow the notion of a crazy Nazi scientist spreading poison to revenge Der Führer's death, but I'm damn certain Graebe's a completely ruthless man who'd think nothing of dumping toxic effluent into the water if it saved him the trouble of disposing of it elsewhere.'

'You have two motives, haven't you, Charles?' Mark laid the photograph on the desk with a slight twinge of revulsion, because Kirk's story had brought a lot of memories back. 'Irish unrest worries you, but you believe Graebe was guilty of those war crimes. You hope that his firm was responsible for chemical pollution so that you can hit back at him in a small way.'

'Perfectly true, Mark.' The general stood up and moved over to a filing cabinet labelled 'Top Secret'. 'To prevent civil unrest is what I'm paid for, but to nail Friend Graebe would give me great personal pleasure. If I can hang a charge of negligence and water pollution round his neck, they'd cancel his work permit and sling the bastard back to Germany. Do you blame me?'

'Not if he was guilty.' Mark watched Kirk produce a key and fit it into the cabinet door. 'As you say, a factory producing synthetic resin must have a lot of waste matter to dispose of and some of it might be toxic. Graebe could have been responsible for the pollution, he would obviously stop dumping when the epidemic among the wildlife became noticed, and he might start up again when the incident is forgotten. But you still haven't told me where I come in.'

'I need a personal approach from you, Mark.' Kirk opened

the steel door. The cabinet might contain secret material, but there was also an impressive array of bottles and glasses on its shelves. 'I want a team of inspectors to go through that factory with a fine-tooth comb. I want them to question all the employees and check every file on record. Graebe won't allow that, but there's someone who can make him open up, and that person is a pal of yours.' Kirk poured out two measures of whisky and soda. 'D.R. Products happens to be a subsidiary company of Rydercraft Aviation.'

'Whose chairman is Daniel Ryder.' Mark fought to control his expression as Kirk handed him a glass. His feelings towards Daniel Ryder were quite irrational and he despised himself for them. Ryder was a cold fish socially, but also a charitable and generous man, and they'd always managed to get along fairly well. Certainly Mark respected him for his drive and ambition. Daniel Ryder had started his career as a lecturer in aerodynamics and then launched into business and built up a modest commercial empire in a few short years. Not so modest either. Probably this chemical plant was just one of many subsidiary companies, and certainly Rydercraft Aviation was a star performer on the export field. Its Skyriders might not be very large or impressive planes, but they were economical and gluttons for punishment, and airlines operated them over most of the world. Ryder had done Mark no personal harm, he was not responsible for what had happened to Tania and the baby, and Mark was a childish fool to harbour any feelings against him.

'I know Ryder,' he said. 'He is my landlord as it happens. Tania and I have a cottage on his estate at Treflys in Wales, and I'll probably see him when we go there for a few days at the end of the month. But he's not a friend, Charles. Not somebody I could ask a favour of.'

'Don't be so damn silly, Mark. Tania told me you were on friendly terms and she also said that you treated Ryder's wife for pneumonia once. If you asked him he might put pressure on Graebe for me.' The general took a swig of whisky and frowned. 'What's the matter? Don't you want to put a stop to further pollution and send a Nazi butcher packing?'

'Naturally I do, but ...' The house telephone rang and Mark broke off as Kirk went to answer it. Why? he asked himself. Just what had caused Tania's accident? Why had an experienced and sober driver lost control of his car? Why ... why ... why?

'Thank you, my dear.' Kirk was speaking to his secretary. 'And also thank God that it's happened here and not in Ireland. If that had been the case, the balloon might be going up this very moment. Now, just repeat what you heard again.' He listened intently and then replaced the instrument.

'Well, Mark,' he said. 'I won't be needing your help after all. Nobody could make Graebe agree to an inspection merely because wildlife suffered from pollution, but the situation has changed and he'll have to open up now.' Kirk laid down his cigar and took another swig of whisky.

'Fish, lobsters and birds died, but not oysters. They were thought to be unaffected by the disease. But they are now and they've passed on their complaint with interest. The Health people have just issued a warning on the radio.' He walked back to the cabinet and refilled his glass.

'This afternoon the Lord Mayor of London gave a luncheon party for a group of foreign industrialists, and it appears that after enjoying a few dozen Linsleat oysters, His Worship, two aldermen, five councillors and nine of their distinguished guests had to leave the table in a hurry.' Kirk gave a wry grin. 'Stomach pumps soon put them off the danger list, but they all exhibited symptoms of severe food poisoning.

'Here's to them, my boy. To the oysters, I mean.' He raised his glass and his smile widened. 'To the little blighters that are going to send Graebe back where he belongs.

'Oh, yes, he's target Number One now.' Kirk knocked back his drink in a single practised movement. 'You see, the power station and D.R. Products are the only organizations that discharge effluent anywhere near the oyster-beds.'

Chapter Two

Treflys valley was funnel-shaped and its scenery so varied that Mark often imagined he was passing through three separate landscapes during the drive from the village. At first the road wound through pasture land that looked more appropriate to Kent or Sussex than North Wales. But after crossing a stream, the terrain steepened and the route ran up between hillocks thickly covered with rhododendron bushes that had an almost tropical appearance when in bloom. Then, beyond the manor house and a series of hairpin bends, the stream was recrossed and the funnel opened out into a wild expanse of fells flanked by scree shoots and old quarry terraces that mounted the hills like gigantic staircases. The quarries had been closed for years; apart from holiday traffic few cars made the climb beyond the manor, and the Levins' cottage and two small farms were the only occupied buildings. But though the area was desolate, there was something very attractive about it, and the views of the Welsh mountains were certainly spectacular. On a clear day the Snowdon range was visible, to the south lay the peaks of Cader Idris, and dominating everything stood the towering hump of Allt y Cnicht, the Hill of the Knight.

'That's the lot, darling.' Mark carried the last bag into the sitting-room. They had had a quick journey from London and it was still only late afternoon.

'Good show.' Since settling in England, Tania Levin had tried to adopt a hearty manner of speech, but it didn't really come off. She had been born Tania Valina Petrovna, citizeness of no mean republic, and her accent clashed dramatically with the jargon of Home Counties suburbia. Her physical appearance was also a dramatic contrast, and was one of the things that had first attracted Mark to her. She was a tall, fair-haired girl with a thin, youthful face topping a maturely developed body, and sometimes she made him think of two women sharing the same house. A soulful madonna upstairs and plump Mother Russia occupying the ground floor and the basement. 'You're glad you came, aren't you?'

'I suppose so. We can both do with a break.' Mark stood in the doorway. Rain had dogged them during the journey, but it had blown over now and the flanks of Allt y Cnicht were bathed in sunlight, though mist still shrouded the jagged summit. Two hundred odd miles away from the mountain was London, and about one hundred miles in the opposite direction lay the Linsleat estuary. A week had passed since the outbreak of food poisoning occurred, and though no further cases had come to light, the authorities had taken quick action. The patients had fully recovered, no traces of a salmonella infection had been found to account for their condition, but the oysters showed an abnormally high iodine content. That could have caused the illness and it also suggested that chemical pollution had affected the creature's metabolisms. A tribunal had been set up, and till its findings were established, D.R. Products must be regarded with deep suspicion. Whether Ryder and Graebe and their shareholders liked it or not, a team of inspectors were at work at the plant and no more of their waste products could be discharged into the estuary. As a compromise they were allowed to transport the effluent out to sea in barges, but that was still a costly operation and Graebe had issued an official protest. Mark agreed with the decision in principle, but was not entirely convinced that the culprits had been found. In spite of the Electricity Board's assurances, he still regarded the nuclear power station as a likely suspect.

How had Daniel Ryder liked the order, he wondered, looking down the slope of the valley to the manor. Ryder's house – 'Miss Megan's house', as everybody called it because

Ryder had married the late squire's daughter – lay hunched in a coppice: an attractive Tudor building with massive stone walls and slate roofs. An imposing property, and Ryder was unkindly rumoured to have married Megan so that he could gain the estate and adopt her father's role. Certainly he played the benevolent landowner with a flourish and had lavished money on the neighbourhood. A new village hall, a cottage hospital, a children's playground, were just a few of his gifts, and when a mining company had sought to prospect for copper to the south of Allt y Cnicht, he had bought them out to preserve the scenic amenities. He had also performed one charitable action which had been deeply resented. Last winter a disused farm-building had been converted into a free hostel for young people, and hairy youths and bedraggled girls drooped despondently around the village, creating local scandal and constantly arousing the suspicions of Constable Ivor Johns: 'Ryder's blasted hippies', who were suspected of drug-taking, thefts of poultry, and every possible sexual indulgence.

Because of this, and also because Ryder's personality was not one to inspire popularity, his role of kindly squire went unappreciated. The people of the valley were clannish and suspicious of strangers, and many of them disliked having an Englishman lording it at the big house. Another man might have won them over, but Daniel Ryder had failed. His neighbours used his hall and his hospital and his playground, they smiled politely at him, but in private he was still considered an interloper, 'that foreigner whom Miss Meg should never have married'.

Mark and Tania knew a good deal about local feeling, because they had broken the ice during their first visit to the area. Old Dr Travers, the G.P., had fractured his collar-bone at the height of an influenza epidemic and Mark had volunteered to help his assistant. He had slogged over the fells to outlying farms and cottages, he had taken surgeries, and he had probably saved Megan Ryder's life when pneumonia set in. This had gained him a footing in the community, but not full membership. Though he and Tania came to Wales several times a year now, they were still regarded as no more than acceptable outsiders, and, like the manor, their cottage went by its former name: 'Roberts's house . . . the old judge's house'.

A difficult people to understand, Mark thought. Very charming, very kind if you didn't rub them up the wrong way, very witty. But so pagan, so morbidly superstitious. They might joke about their local folklore, but there was always a false ring in the laughter. Especially when they mentioned Daran: a legendary being said to have ruled the area before their Celtic ancestors arrived. When Maggie Owen's temperature had shot up to a hundred and four she had clutched Mark's hand and told him that she wanted to die before 'the old ones', the hill demons, came down from Allt y Cnicht to fetch her. Miss Owen was the hard-bitten mother of five, each fathered by a different partner, and she was said to make a living by organizing parties at which cockfights and her three teenage daughters provided rival entertainments. When she recovered from the flu, Maggie had chuckled about her ravings, but Mark knew that she had believed every word that was screamed out at him.

'Roberts's house . . . the old judge's house.' He walked back into the cottage. Tania had gone upstairs to unpack and he looked around the sitting-room and the kitchen beyond it. Tania and a local builder had made a wonderful job of the conversion. An Aga stove had replaced the original cast-iron grate, the flagstone floor was covered with parquet and rugs, the oak beams and uprights were screened behind plasterboard, the furniture was modern. But, as often happened when he was alone, Mark saw the building as it had once been, and felt the presence of its former owner.

Mr Justice Roberts, the old judge, Treflys's most famous

son. A hanging judge, if ever there was, who had retired from the bench on the day capital punishment was abolished, claiming that his job had been made a mockery. Roberts had been born in the cottage and he returned there to study local history, write his memoirs and die. He died all right, but the memoirs were never completed. When his daily woman found him one morning, he had recently written the heading for Chapter Twelve: 'Marston and Kerr, the Brighton poisoners – Two evil men who should have gone to the scaffold'. A publisher would have queried that chapter for libel because the men involved were acquitted, but the heading was all that there was and the rest of the page was blank. While the judge was at work, somebody had crept into the cottage and knocked him unconscious. Somebody had bound his hands and wrists together. Somebody had waited for him to recover consciousness and then held his face to the fire till he died of heart failure.

Somebody who was never caught, though suspects were legion. Roberts had been notorious for his savage sentences, and plenty of law-breakers and their friends had reason to hate him. One of them must have tortured the old man to death, but he left no clues and the judge lay unavenged in Treflys churchyard.

We couldn't live here, Mark thought. It's fine for holidays, for a week or ten days, but impossible as a home. He considered what the cottage had been like when he and Tania first visited it with the estate agent. The smell of damp and mustiness, the dark paint and woodwork, the 'Spy' legal cartoons on the sitting-room walls, and in the judge's bedroom steel engravings cut from an illustrated edition of Dante's *Inferno,* all depicting the torments of the damned. Roberts's robes were still hanging in the wardrobe and a sampler over the bed proclaimed 'What a terrible thing it is to fall into the hands of the Living God.' The spare bedroom had been used as a library, and it gave a fine character-study of the former occupant.

Legal volumes and works on local history and folklore filled most of the shelves, but other books were more revealing. *The City of God* of Saint Augustine rubbed shoulders with Pascal's *Pensées,* Calvin's *Institutio* stood beside a profusely illustrated copy of *God's Revenge against Murder,* and wedged among a collection of Victorian tracts was a personal memento: a scrap-book filled with press cuttings of the judge's cases and fifteen photographs with black crosses inked over them. One or two of the subjects seemed familiar, and after a time Mark realized who they were. The book was a kind of butterfly collection and each crossed-out photograph showed the face of a murderer Mr Justice Roberts had sentenced to death. The cottage was once the home of a man obsessed with the punishment of evil, and Mark and Tania had thought twice about buying the lease. But they had fallen in love with the valley, the agent had pointed out what modernization could do and at last Mark had produced his cheque-book.

The dogs at the upper farm had been barking since they arrived and another sound had joined them. The characteristic exhaust note of a Skyrider pulsing over the hills, with its strange modulated beat which seemed almost rhythmic. Mark crossed to the window and scowled as he saw the aircraft circle the valley. The blasted things were everywhere and there was no escape from them. He heard them at his laboratory, they flew over his house at Richmond, and this one would be on a test flight from Rydercraft's factory at Llancir. Wherever he went, that eerie engine beat would remind him of his loss.

As the plane vanished over the slopes of Allt y Cnicht he pictured what had happened. A suburban street leading down to the Thames, a car slowing for a pedestrian-crossing. Tania – eight months pregnant – stepping down from the kerb. And as she did so, a low-flying Skyrider had appeared over the rooftops and the car had shot forward.

The driver, a salesman named Michael Turner, was quite sober and he had a clean licence. He claimed that the sudden noise had distracted him and he had mistaken the accelerator pedal for the brake; but the defence was not accepted. Part of Turner's sales territory was around London Airport and he must have experienced low-flying aircraft several times a day. The magistrates were lenient, however. They considered that overwork was the main contributing factor and Turner must have dozed off. He was fined eighty pounds and lost his licence for a year. Tania lost her baby – it was delivered still-born in the ambulance – and there was small chance that she could ever have another.

'Mark, please don't look like that.' He turned and saw Tania coming down the stairs. 'Your face just then . . . you looked haunted.

'Oh, darling, does it still mean so much to you after thirteen months? If you really want a child badly let's adopt one.'

'No adoption, my sweet.' He stepped forward and put his arms around her. 'Being a Yid I have a craving for personal parentage. The desire that my seed shall people the earth. A disgusting ambition, so let's forget it.' He kissed her on the mouth and then grinned sourly. 'Sorry about the wounded-stag expression, but whenever I hear one of those bloody air-craft I keep thinking how wonderful things might have been.'

'I've kept thinking about it too, Mark. You know that well enough.' Tania drew back and shook her head. 'Not only about the baby but about Turner. The medical report showed he was quite healthy and though he may have been tired, his story was that the aircraft made him lose control of the car. I just can't understand it, you know. A good, experienced driver being so startled by a sudden noise that he mistook an accelerator for a brake.

'But, as you said, let's forget it and have a Scotch. I could certainly use one.' Tania looked down at the cartons they had brought from London and grimaced. 'Hell! What a fool I am. I remember packing the drinks, but I must have left the box behind. How about going down to the local?'

'That's fine by me, but what's the time?' Mark fought back a frown as he glanced at his watch. Daniel Ryder often visited the pub during the early evening and he didn't really want to meet him. Thinking about his child's death had brought back the ridiculous feeling that Ryder, as manufacturer and chief designer of the aircraft, was somehow to blame. How crazy can emotion make one?

'Yes, they should be open when we get there, so let's go.'

He pushed the notion of Ryder's responsibility out of his mind and led the way to the door.

It was a pleasant evening, clear and bright, and after the recent rain the countryside was glistening in the sunlight. As he drove down the lane to the village, Mark's reluctance to meet Daniel Ryder vanished and he began to hope that they would find him at the inn. Ryder was a proud man and said to be very ruthless where business was concerned. He was also half Jewish and the fact that he had employed Graebe, an ex-Nazi suspected of war crimes, proved his ruthlessness. It would be interesting to see how such a man reacted to the enforced inspection of his plant. Would he show anxiety that something was amiss at D.R. Products, or would he consider himself victimized? Probably the latter. In spite of official assurances, the power station was a very possible source of the pollution.

There was the manor house below them. Mark smiled at the view. A very nice house indeed, set well back in a coppice and surrounded by trim lawns and gardens. A car was moving along the drive, which joined the road at a corner, and he prepared to slow down and let it pass in front of him. He was still smiling when the car emerged from the gates: a Ford Cortina with a single occupant. He reached for the brake pedal; then his smile died, his foot slid sideways, the sky went dark and he heard Tania scream.

When Mark opened his eyes the Ford was out of sight, but he knew that he had not been mistaken. No freak of imagination had caused his blackout and made him ram their own car against a wall. Sudden shock was responsible and he had seen the driver's face quite clearly. As clearly as he had seen it in the magistrate's court. The man who had killed Tania's baby was back on the road and he had been visiting Daniel Ryder.

Chapter 3

'My dear chap, I can't tell you how sorry I am. Such a shocking thing to have happened.' Daniel Ryder spoke with sympathy and embarrassment, but the side of his face that was turned towards Mark could not express much emotion. The nose had been broken and badly set and the muscles of the left cheek and eyelid were partially paralysed. He was a keen rock climber and Mark seemed to remember hearing that a fall in the French Alps had caused his injuries.

'Yes, a most unfortunate coincidence that you should have run across Turner, but I had no idea that you were coming to Treflys today. If I had known you were due, I'd have made quite certain that your paths did not cross.'

'I'm sure you would, Daniel.' Mark nodded. The two men were pacing the garden while the Ryders' chauffeur-handyman, Willie Price, attended to the car. It was lucky that a burst tyre was the only damage; Willie was said to be a loyal retainer and devoted to Megan, but he did not look like a mechanical genius. A massive, ungainly youth whom Mark suspected to be feeble-minded. Certainly he was immensely strong, and three fun-loving louts who had once tried to give him the boot after a football match had all ended up in hospital.

'But what is the connection between you and Turner, Daniel?' Mark could hear snatches of conversation drifting towards them from the summer-house where Megan Ryder was entertaining Tania and two guests. One was Cedric Brag-

shaw, a director of Rydercraft Aviation, whom the Levins had
met before, and the other an American professor of history
named John Rushton. Tania had no idea that Turner had been
driving the Ford. Mark had told her that a beam of sunlight
had blinded him, but he had taken Ryder aside at the first
opportunity. 'I'm rather surprised that you should be on social
terms with someone who knocked down my wife and killed
her child.'

'Social terms? You've got it all wrong, Mark. Turner is just
an employee. He works at one of our subsidiary companies
and I certainly don't know him socially.' Ryder wore an old
tweed jacket with fishing flies stuck in the lapels, and a pair
of corduroy slacks. It had often occurred to Mark that he was
a man who enjoyed playing several roles, and at the moment
the country squire act was very much in evidence. An act that
was not really a success, however. Before entering commerce
Ryder had been first a don, a lecturer in aerodynamics at a red-
brick university, and then a civil servant. Joined together with
the battered face and the shabby clothes were the mixed auras
of scholarship, clericalism and business acumen.

'You gave him a job, Daniel.' Mark raised his eyebrows.
'You must have known Michael Turner was responsible for
Tania's accident – the case was widely reported – yet you
employed him.'

'I employed Turner because of the accident, Mark.' Ryder
stopped pacing and turned his head. The other side of his face
had escaped damage and it clashed grotesquely with the rigid
mask of its partner. 'After his trial Turner contacted me and
said that he had been sacked by his firm and was at a loose end.
I offered him a job because I felt sorry for him and also partly
responsible . . .'

'Responsible?' He had paused and Mark prompted him.
'You felt responsible for the accident?'

'Yes, Mark, I did. A most neurotic view, but it bothered
me for some time. There's no denying that those Model III

Skyriders had a bad sonic vibration, which has since been rectified, and the pilot was making a very low landing approach to London Airport. I kept telling myself that, as the manufacturer of the aircraft, I had personally contributed to your child's death, and Michael Turner was also a victim. Once or twice I thought of letting you know my feelings, but it seemed unkind to bring the matter up.

'Also, you wouldn't have understood them. So absurd, such a nonsensical guilt. As the magistrate said, Turner lost control of his car because he was overtired. If he'd had his wits about him, the plane would never have startled him and Tania's baby would be alive.'

'I do understand your feelings, Daniel, and thank you for telling me.' Mark's own feelings were of release. Somehow it was a relief to know that Ryder had shared his delusion that he was partly to blame for what had happened. His bitterness towards Turner had also vanished. He himself had lost control of his car because of a sudden shock, and if there had been another child on the way it might also have died. 'I'm sorry I brought the matter up, but I had to know your relationship with Turner.'

'Naturally you did.' Ryder sighed. 'Why are coincidences usually unpleasant? Today, of all days, one of our executives has to send me some material from Northern Ireland, he picks Turner as his delivery boy and your paths cross. All most unfortunate.'

'From Northern Ireland?' Willie Price had changed the wheel and Mark watched him turn the car into the drive. 'Turner works at Linsleat?'

'Yes, Mark. He is employed as clerical assistant to Hans Graebe, my head man there, and you and I are going to have a chat about that Linsleat business, I hope. I understand that the Ministry consulted you as an independent expert.' The genial squire had vanished and there was a resentful gleam in Ryder's sound eye. 'Did you advise them to put us in the pillory?'

'Nothing of the kind, Daniel. I was merely asked to check their analysis that the outbreak of food poisoning at the Mansion House was not caused by a bacteriological or viral infection. I confirmed that that was the case and my responsibility ended.'

'I see.' Ryder nodded, but he did not look entirely convinced. 'Well, let's rejoin the others and have a drink. I'm sure you could use one.' He led the way across the lawn.

'. . . ruddy past president of the Rock Climbers' Club, but he came a cropper on an easy scramble and bust his thigh.' The sound of talking became louder as they approached the summer-house; Cedric Bragshaw, a thick-set, boisterous man and, like Ryder, a keen mountaineer, was holding forth. 'And do you know how the old fool did it, Meg? Funniest thing since the Bishop of Lanchester fell off the Matterhorn.' The voice boomed with glee. 'Slipped on a banana skin some damned hiker had dropped on the Snowdon Horseshoe.'

'It would be a great privilege if you and your good gentleman would visit our camp, Lady Levin.' Professor Rushton's pleasant Boston accent gave Tania's title due deference. 'We are fifteen in number, all amateurs apart from myself, and we are drawn from several age groups, nationalities and walks of life. The site is a veritable Tower of Babel, in fact.'

'Everybody else has a full glass, so what about us, Meg?' Ryder motioned Mark towards a deck-chair. 'Scotch and water isn't it, old boy, and I'll have a gin and bitters.

'Not too much bitters, though, my dear. You usually make them look like blood.' Ryder's heartiness was obviously forced and Mark watched his wife obey him. Megan was small and slightly built, with restless eyes and a deceptively mild manner that hid great strength of character. When Mark treated her for pneumonia he had rarely seen a patient fight illness with such tenacity. She was much younger than her husband, and gossip had it that he rarely shared her bed and she found solace elsewhere.

If that was correct, Mark didn't really blame her, because Meg had had an unhappy life. Her family had owned land around Treflys for centuries and regarded themselves as something akin to feudal overlords. But death duties and unwise investments and the decline of the slate industry had finally ruined them and the crash came suddenly. Her father had shot himself on the day he was declared bankrupt, and Meg had married Ryder a month later. Rumour stated that she had accepted him to preserve the estate and stave off its creditors, but whatever the truth, there appeared to be little love between them now.

'Professor Rushton is an archaeologist, Mark. Just fancy that.' Tania made the occupation sound exotic in the extreme. 'He and his party are camped to the north of Allt y Cnicht and they are digging for Celtic remains.'

'Not Celtic remains, Lady Levin, I thought I had made that quite clear.' Rushton had unruly white hair that stirred as he shook his head. 'We hope to find evidence of a civilization that flourished in this area long before the Celts – or Gaels, to give them their correct name – appeared in the British Isles, Sir Marcus.'

'But you won't, old boy, because such a civilization never existed.' Bragshaw guffawed loudly. 'Those legends about a lost tribe who were ruled by priest-kings and had supernatural powers are all my eye and Betty Martin. Romantic yarns like Gelert's grave and Arthur's sword. The Welsh are an inventive lot who love spinning yarns, and, saving your presence, Meg, dead superstitious.'

'Thank you, Cedric.' Though he was a boorish person, Bragshaw had not meant to be rude, but Marcus saw Megan flush as she handed him his glass. 'And we are not only superstitious, but dullards. As my husband often remarks, the Welsh pride themselves on being a talented race, but all they produce are actors, singers and rubbishy radical politicians.'

'We have not been able to gather much information locally,

Mr Bragshaw.' There had been an unpleasant pause and
Rushton resumed the topic. 'When we first arrived, people
thought we were tourists and they seemed friendly and quite
ready to answer our questions. But as soon as they realized
we were serious investigators, they changed. They became
reticent, even hostile, and their attitude persuades me that
our mission will be successful. The people of Treflys's silence
is confirmation that we have come to the right place. They
not only believe the legend of an ancient civilization that
was wiped out by their ancestors; they are terrified of it.' He
nodded towards Allt y Cnicht. The mist had blown away and
the summit loomed over the valley looking exactly like the
helmet of some vast stone warrior. 'Isn't it true that farmers
will not graze sheep or cattle on the northern slopes of that
mountain, Mr Ryder?'

'Perfectly true, but our peasants are not alone in being
superstitious witch hunters.' Ryder reached in his pocket and
held out a sheet of foolscap. 'Do you agree that this is just and
fair, Mark?'

'I'm afraid I do.' The sheet was a Photostat of the order for-
bidding D.R. Products to discharge any waste materials into
the Linsleat estuary till the inquiry was completed. 'Your firm
and the power station were the only establishments releasing
effluent near the oyster-beds, and the oysters had suffered
some glandular disturbance which produced an abnormal
iodine content in their systems. People who ate them became
ill and three patients nearly died. Surely you admit that pollution must be responsible?'

'I'll go further than that.' Ryder had emptied his glass and
nodded for Meg to refill it. 'Of course there was pollution, but
why pick on us? I agree that we and the power station have
discharged effluent near the oyster-beds, but you may possibly have heard that water is not a solid substance that remains
static in one position. Hell's bells, that estuary is tidal, Mark,
and there's a fair-sized river flowing into it. Currents could

have washed the poison from several sources; it could have drifted in from the sea, if it comes to that. So why have we been selected as the obvious villains?'

'Because ours is the only concern which refused to cooperate, old boy.' Bragshaw broke in before Mark could reply. 'Had we agreed to an inspection after the early epidemic among the birds and fish was noticed, there'd have been no unpleasantness. But if you must employ an arrogant squarehead like Graebe and he refuses to give an inch, what do you expect?'

'Hans Graebe may appear arrogant, Cedric, but he is a first-class chemist and businessman and that's why I put him in charge of the plant.' Ryder turned coldly away from Bragshaw and looked at Mark. 'When the original request for an inspection arrived we ... Graebe, that is, was working on a new formula for the production of synthetic fibres, and not unnaturally he feared a leakage of information to our competitors. The process has now been patented and we have nothing to hide. We welcome the inspection, but I regard an order that forces us to transport our waste materials out to sea as victimization. You will remember, Mark, that we gave the strongest possible assurances that no toxic effluent was being discharged by us in sufficient quantity to harm any living creature.'

'I saw that statement, Daniel, but assurances and proof are different things. Why should anybody accept the word of – '

'I thought that would come up.' Mark had been about to say 'the word of an interested party', but Ryder interrupted him angrily. 'The word of a man who was accused of war crimes twenty-six years ago. For your information Graebe was acquitted on every count and I know he was innocent. I know it as surely as I know my own name. My mother was a Jewess, Mark. Do you think I'd have given a key job to a Nazi butcher?'

'You might have done, if you had a forgiving nature.' Graebe must have a curious personality, Mark thought. In spite of the lack of evidence, Charles Kirk had been quite sure the man was a war criminal who got away with his crimes. 'I could sense his guilt across the court-room,' he had said. Kirk was astute and perceptive, but so was Ryder and he had complete faith in the German's innocence. 'After the war another Jew, Victor Gollancz, stated that we should forgive the Germans, Daniel.'

'I have not got a forgiving nature, Mark, but I pride myself on being a judge of character. When Hans Graebe assured me that we were not responsible for the Linsleat pollution, I accepted his word as that of a man of honour and a highly competent scientist.

'Just a moment, though.' Ryder paused, and it was clear that his anger had died as quickly as it had flared up. 'Meg, please go to my study and bring out the container that ... that Graebe's assistant delivered.' He had been about to name Michael Turner, but must have remembered Tania's ignorance. 'You'll find it on the desk, my dear. Looks rather like a small vacuum-flask.

'But the authorities won't have to accept our assurances much longer, Mark. Three Ministry inspectors are on our premises, and samples of effluent have been sent to the public analyst. We'll be exonerated soon enough, but how can you believe that I'd have refused an inquiry if there was any doubt about our innocence? I'm very fond of animals, and I'd have stopped production if there was the slightest chance we were responsible for such suffering.' Ryder stared up at the sky with a faraway look in his eyes. The squire and the aggrieved businessman had vanished and a soulful nature-lover was on stage.

'No, D.R. Products were not to blame for the pollution and this will prove it.' His wife had come back into the summer-house and handed him a plastic container. As he had said, it was rather like a vacuum-flask and the stopper was heavily sealed.

'Here's your suspect, Mark. A sample of effluent from our plant taken by Ministry of Health inspectors and diluted three times with saline solution. On entering the estuary it would naturally have been diluted several thousand times.' He held out the seal for Mark's inspection, then laid down the flask and finished his gin and angostura.

'My friends, would you like a demonstration? Analysis will clear our name soon enough, but what about the present? Shall I show you how completely I trust Hans Graebe?' Ryder broke the seal, removed the stopper and poured a measure of greenish-grey liquid into his glass.

'Skip the dramatics, Dan.'

'Don't be a bloody fool.'

'Mr Ryder, I really do beg you . . .'

Bragshaw and Mark and Professor Rushton simultaneously voiced their protests, Tania leaned anxiously forward, and only Megan appeared unworried. Quite the opposite. Her eyes were riveted on the glass as if willing him to drink from it.

'You don't want me to prove my point with an experiment?' Ryder smiled from one face to another. 'If this effluent is what you seem to suspect, Mark, I have a great deal to answer for. Surely it is only fair that I sample its qualities? All you have to do is ask me.'

'I don't give a damn what you do, but I'm tired of play-acting.' Mark stood up and motioned Tania to do the same. When Ryder poured out the liquid, he had felt anxiety. If that effluent was the source of contamination, it had produced disease, deformity and death in animals, and several human beings had become violently ill because they had eaten shell-fish infected by it. For a moment he had considered knocking the glass from Ryder's hand; but now he knew that there was no need, and his anxiety was replaced by irritation. Ryder was an exhibitionist, a poseur. He was confident no one would ask him to drink from the glass and he had never had the slightest intention of doing so. The whole business was an act to impress and Mark had had enough of it. 'Thank you for your hospitality and we'll be on our way.'

'Please don't go, Mark and Tania, because I do give a damn.' Megan barred their way, still looking towards her husband. 'We've been offered a demonstration and I want to witness it. Go on, Dan. Drink up like a good boy and show us how blameless you and Graebe are. Pretty please, Dan.'

'Thank you, my dear, devoted wife.' The words were a curse, Ryder's hand was shaking as he raised the glass and Mark saw how pathetically the performance would end. The tremor was feigned, he would spill the liquid before it came anywhere near his mouth and explain away the accident on bad nerves. Meg had forced the actor to face humiliation, but there would be no risk to his health.

'Go on, Dan. I challenge you.' There was both a plea and a sneer in Meg's lilting voice. 'Drink up and prove your faith in Graebe.'

'Very well. Here goes and when you're satisfied that I trust Hans completely, we'll pay a visit to the pub and make ourselves really ill on warm, weak, watery Welsh beer.

'Cheers, Meg.' Ryder spat out the toast, but the tremor had stopped and Mark knew he was wrong. He lunged towards him, but he was too late. Before he could reach the glass Ryder had swallowed the effluent.

Chapter Four

'You are sure that you washed them carefully, both the glass and the container?' Once the demonstration was over Ryder's nervous manner had left him and he smiled mockingly as Meg came back to the summer-house. 'Thank you, my dear. We'll know soon enough whether my confidence is justified, but I might be wrong and one shouldn't leave dangerous poison

lying about, eh?' He had patted her shoulder and beamed at
his guests. 'Now, with the Linsleat sewage disposed of, let's go
and sample the local variety.'

Just what was the truth? Mark wondered, as he sipped at
his drink in the pub. Had Ryder been really worried and had
Meg's pleas forced him to raise the glass to his lips? Or was
he completely sure that the effluent was non-toxic and no
harm could come to him? Mark watched the man through the
smoke of the saloon bar. Were the show of nerves and the
trembling hand just stage props to give dramatic effect? Had
Daniel Ryder wanted to play the part of the brave man risking
his life for an act of faith?

In any case, he had suffered no ill effects so far and appeared
to have proved his point. Mark could see the church clock
through the window facing him. The people who fell ill at the
Mansion House banquet had done so within a few minutes
of eating the oysters, but over half an hour had passed since
Ryder drank the effluent. There could be a delayed action on
the way, but Mark doubted that. No matter what D.R. Products had discharged in the past, their present waste materials
must be harmless and Ryder's confidence in Graebe had been
justified.

But whatever the truth on that point, Mark noticed that
Daniel Ryder's unpopularity seemed to have increased since
their last visit to Treflys. Mark and Tania were sitting with Professor Rushton at a corner table, Megan was at the bar talking
to old Dr Travers and a farmer named Emrys Hughes, and
Ryder was moving around the room trying to make himself
agreeable. His greetings and small talk about crops and the
weather were acknowledged politely but without warmth,
and as soon as he passed on, his tenants resumed their conver-
sations in Welsh.

The Rose and Leek, generally referred to as the Leak, was
an old, rambling public house and the only one within miles,
though Treflys supported a church, three chapels, a cinema-

cum-bingo hall and a good selection of small shops. One of
the chapels stood beside the church, and a group of men and
boys were filing out from choir practice. Mark noticed that
they all kept their eyes averted from three young men and a
girl lounging against the churchyard wall: four of Ryder's hippies looking out of place and unhappy.

However, though his protégés might be resented, they
could not be the main reason for Ryder's unpopularity. The
Leak was a pleasant pub, Mark and Tania usually enjoyed a
drink there, and this evening their welcome had been particularly warm. They had arrived a few minutes before the
Ryders and Rushton – Bragshaw had remained behind to
write letters – and had been greeted with nods and smiles
from almost everyone in the bar. Dr Travers had leered lech-
erously at Tania and complimented her on her appearance,
Emrys Hughes had taken Mark's hand in a crushing grip, even
Mary Ellis, the usually remorseful landlady, had been jovial.
But once Ryder appeared, the atmosphere altered. Megan was
obviously regarded with deep respect and affection, but her
husband shared neither. There had been a hush when he came
into the room and Mark could see veiled dislike in the face of
each man and woman he spoke to.

The curious thing was that Ryder appeared to be oblivious
of the feelings he aroused, and he moved around the bar with
a courteous word for everyone. A democratic landowner
at ease with his inferiors, though not a very considerate
employer. His Rolls-Royce was parked outside and Mark
could see Willie Price slouched behind the steering wheel.
Surely a true squire would have brought him in for a drink or
sent him to get a cup of tea?

'Brownies and gnomes, Lady Levin. Leprechauns, trolls
and pixies. The tradition of a small, secretive race hiding out
in the hills is common to much of Western Europe.' Professor
Rushton was on his hobby-horse again. 'In some cases they are
regarded as mischievous, but lovable; in others, malevolent.

But all accounts agree that they are an alien species, stunted, malformed and socially unacceptable.

'But there is also a tradition that a highly organized society flourished in these parts during the late Neolithic era, and it is my conviction that these hill people – pixies, leprechauns, whatever the local name may be – were the last units of this civilization. Degenerates who had lost their vitality over the ages, possibly through miscegenation with their more primitive neighbours, who later destroyed them.' The professor appeared to think he was back in the lecture room, and Mark saw Tania stifle a yawn.

'There are numerous legends to support this theory, they differ considerably in detail, but they all confirm these people's early attainments. Lack of architectural remains – buildings, burial places and so forth – suggests that they were nomads, but they worked bronze and iron, had developed a legal system and a runic alphabet, and practised mono-theism.' John Rushton ticked off the attainments on fingers which were as horny as a labourer's. Though leader of the archaeologists, he obviously did his fair share of the digging.

'But without architectural evidence, how can you possibly know all this, Professor?' Mark watched Ryder return to the bar and order another pint of beer. He still appeared to be perfectly healthy and there could have been nothing toxic in the effluent. D.R. Products seemed to be in the clear and the authorities would have to find another source of the Linsleat pollution. 'Is your whole theory based on folklore and tradition?'

'Mainly, Sir Marcus, but don't sneer at tradition. Much of our great Christian ethic rests on little else.' Rushton spoke with a cherry-wood pipe clenched between his teeth. He was deeply tanned and his shrewd blue eyes and unruly white hair made Mark think of a character out of *Bonanza*: old grandpappy, the champion of the homesteaders, who'd spot the baddies when they clattered into town and saddle up to summon Lorne Greene.

'Apart from the nomadic theory and the time factors, the lack of building remains is easily accounted for. Before their decline these people had been hated and feared by the Gaelic invaders, and after military defeat they were massacred and as far as possible all traces of their existence obliterated.

'There is some material evidence available, of course. Dr Ian Clarkson, a compatriot of mine, who visited the area in 1939, collected examples of pottery and bronze work which were definitely not Gaelic or Neolithic in origin. There was also a local scholar, Mr Justice Roberts, who published a monograph in which he claimed to have deciphered a portion of the runic alphabet used by these people.'

'Judge Roberts ... our predecessor at the cottage?' Tania was curious. 'I heard he was interested in local history, but I never knew he published anything about it.'

'The book was privately printed after his death.' Ryder joined them at the table. 'The title was *The Watcher of the Hills,* but as with his memoirs it was never completed. Such a pity. Roberts's information would have been invaluable. He once told me that he had located the runic inscriptions on a carved stone slab. He wouldn't say where, but he claimed to have translated some of the text and suspected he knew where Daran was buried.'

'Daran?'

Tania had questioned Ryder, but the professor answered. 'Daran, Lady Levin, was the name adopted by all the leaders of that ancient race and their nature is variously described. The Gaels considered them to be demons, but to their followers they were priests and kings, prophets and law-givers with divine powers. One version of the legend has it that they were a single immortal being passing through successive human bodies.

'As might be expected, Judge Roberts believed in the diabolical element of the story, and in his opinion the massacre of the people was justified. "A necessary cleansing operation to wipe out a tainted species devoted to evil and the works of the devil" was one phrase he used.'

'I can imagine him writing that.' Like Mark, Tania sometimes felt the judge's aura in the cottage and she remembered the scrap-book and the crossed-out faces of the men he had sent to the gallows. 'He must have been obsessed with evil.'

'He was quite mad, Tania; superstitious, savage, embittered. In another age Roberts would have excelled himself as a burner of witches.' Ryder glanced towards his wife, who was still at the bar with Dr Travers and Emrys Hughes. 'All the same, it is a great shame that he never finished his book or revealed where that runic inscription is located. Would have made your work much easier, Professor.'

'Much easier, but we will manage without his help, Mr Ryder.' Rushton's eyes were fixed on the window and the plunging flanks of Allt y Cnicht. 'Several mountains are said to be the sacred hill of Daran and the old people, but I am persuaded that that is the one, and already we are gathering evidence to prove it. Very soon we are bound to find definite information which will lead us to the actual burial place.' He turned to Mark. 'And let me repeat how delighted we would all be if you and your good lady care to visit the site of our operations, Sir Marcus.'

'You are very kind, Professor.' Mark replied automatically, but he had hardly been listening. Something was distracting him and he looked around the room to see what it was.

Four young men at the dartboard had stopped their game, Mary Ellis stood with a polished glass in her hand, everyone was staring towards Rushton and nobody was talking. Apart from their group at the table, not a word had been said for a full half-minute and it was the silence that had puzzled him.

'Ah, you are interested in what I was saying, ladies and gentlemen.' Rushton had noticed the stares and he smiled around the room. 'That is excellent, because local beliefs are invaluable aids to archaeology and I would so much like to hear about yours.' He puffed at his pipe and nodded affably to Emrys Hughes.

'You are a farmer, I understand, sir. May I know exactly why you and your colleagues do not graze animals on the northern slopes of Allt y Cnicht?'

For a moment Emrys did not answer and Tania fancied that he was going to put down his unfinished pint of Guinness and stalk out of the room. Then very slowly his mouth curled and the flesh around his eyes crinkled. She could almost share his concentration as he forced himself to smile back at Rushton.

'Colleagues . . . colleagues you call 'em, sir?' He grinned at the men by the dartboard. That's a good 'un, eh, Dai? I work my land with my son, sir, and I have no colleagues. Only competitors . . . enemies like. Fellows who'd steal my sheep and drive off my cattle if I gave 'em half a chance.' Emrys was widely respected as a lay preacher, but he was not as good an actor as Ryder. His humour was clearly forced and his eyes hostile in the crinkled flesh. All the same, he had given a lead and chuckles rang through the room.

'But you are quite right in saying we do not graze beasts on the north of that bastard.' He jerked his thumb in the direction of the mountain. 'Animals are our livelihood, sir; valuable possessions, and we don't want to lose 'em, do we now? We are frightened that those old hill people you were talking about will get 'em. That the sleeping demon will wake up and carry the poor flamers away to his cave.' He took a pull at his stout and behind the counter Mrs Ellis gave a mirthless cackle.

'No, seriously, sir, you're wasting your time. There's no demons, there never was any ancient civilization, but we like a good yarn and that mountain is a ruddy death-trap. The rock is rotten in places and it'll come away at a touch. Riddled with caves and bogs and pitfalls the lower slopes are, and crawling with adders, too. That's why we give it a wide berth and keep the stock fenced off. Ain't that right, lads?' He waited for a murmur of agreement to die down.

'Aye, old Allt y Cnicht herself is the only demon in these parts, and she's a right bitch of a mountain, as you'll learn for yourself if you go on digging into her, sir. A monstrosity, a natural freak, one might say. Where else do you find limestone formations rubbing shoulders with slate and granite? Three chaps were killed by falling rocks when they tried to mine asbestos just after the war, and there've been countless accidents to climbers and hikers.'

'Come off it, Emrys Hughes.' Ryder rapped the table with his glass. 'We all know that the north face is loose and dangerous and that there have been unfortunate accidents, which is why the County Council have put up notices warning people off. But it's not just the physical dangers that frighten you, is it, and I want you to tell Professor Rushton the truth. What do you really think about the mountain?'

'Always ready to obey the squire, Mr Ryder.' Emrys stressed the title contemptuously. 'But why pick on me, gentlemen? I'm an ill-educated man and I know nothing about history . . . prehistory would be the correct term, I suppose, Professor. Why not ask the scholars among the company? Mrs Ellis is a great reader, ain't you, Mary? Or what about the doctor here? He's only a bloody Englishman, but he's lived in Treflys for forty years and gone native – more fool he.'

'Thank you for a mixed compliment, Emrys.' George Travers was a small, leathery-faced man, with an expression which was usually full of mischief. He wore an apple-green anorak and sat perched on the bar stool with his feet off the ground. If it had been an oversized toadstool he would have made an excellent model for a book illustrator. A forest gnome waiting to ensnare the lost traveller, in one of the Grimms' grimmer fairy-tales. 'When you mentioned pixies and so forth just now. Professor Rushton, a children's song came to my mind and I wonder if I can remember how it goes.' The doctor was drinking brandy; he motioned Mrs Ellis to pour him another, and then recited:

' "Up the airy mountain,
    Down the rushy glen.
    We daren't go a-hunting
    For fear of little men."

' "For fear of little men" is rather appropriate to what you've been saying, but fear is a pretty loose term, isn't it? We're anxious about money, worried about health, frightened by physical dangers, but we're only horrified by the unknown. If a tiger came through the doorway I'd be scared for my skin because I'd recognize the creature and know that it could tear me to pieces. But if something unknown entered the room . . . something quite outside my experience, but which I sensed was hostile towards me – call it an evil spirit if you like – I'd be in a state of terror – I'd be petrified.' Travers sniffed thoughtfully over his brandy balloon.

'Yes, we're a superstitious lot who pretend to laugh at our folk-tales to stop strangers laughing at us, but several highly intelligent people have considered that there is something outlandish about the Knight's Hill. Take Mr Justice Roberts, for example. Not the most tolerant human being, but an extremely able one, and he also claimed to be a bit of a clairvoyant. He once said that certain malefactors carried an aura of evil with them and that he could sense this as a terrier can smell out a rat. He also said that he had felt such an aura on the mountain.

'Maybe he was boasting, but if you're so eager for information, why bother with ignoramuses like us?' The doctor had appeared serious for a moment, but now his eyes had a malicious twinkle. 'What advice would you give the professor, Emrys Hughes?'

'There's only one piece of advice to give, as I see it, Doctor.' Hughes grinned back at him and then looked at a painting over the fireplace which depicted the playground and social hall that Ryder had donated to the village. 'You'd like to know how the judge intended to finish his book about the Daran story, so why not devote your energies to finding out, Professor? It shouldn't be difficult for a man of your experience, and if you're short of labour you could ask some of the dropouts from Mr Ryder's hostel to lend you a hand.' He looked Rushton full in the face and his smile widened. 'Take your shovels to the churchyard, dig old Roberts up, and ask him.'

'You bastard, Hughes.' There had been a roar of laughter, but it had not drowned the sharp crack as the glass shattered in Ryder's hand. 'You're a bastard too, Travers; you prompted him. All of you are bastards – ignorant, ungrateful vermin.' He got up and stood swaying before them and his face was almost as red as the blood dribbling from the cut in his palm.

'When I think what I've done for you . . . the money that I've squandered on this miserable village, the . . .' Abuse kept pouring out, but nobody answered him back. Emrys Hughes had ordered another Guinness, the doctor had turned and was facing the bar, the darts game had been resumed. However much Ryder stormed, he might have been dumb and invisible for all the attention that was paid to him.

'Let's get the hell out of here, Rushton. Are you coming, Mark and Tania, or do you intend to stay in this sty?' He pushed past them and clutched his wife's arm. 'And you, Meg. just for once you're going to support me.'

'Whatever you say, Daniel.' For an instant she had drawn towards Emrys as if for protection, and then she shrugged. 'Shall we go, then?'

She spoke quite normally, but as they moved to the door, her sleeve reddening from the grasp of his bleeding hand, Marcus studied her expression and realized that something he had briefly suspected and immediately banished from his mind was true. When Meg prompted Ryder to drink the effluent she had hoped that it might contain enough poison to kill him.

★　　★　　★

Only a quarter to two. Tania was in the kitchen of their cottage and she scowled at the clock. They had had a miserable, embarrassing evening and now it was being followed by a sleepless night. She filled a kettle and put it on the stove. Aspirin and a cup of tea might help, though she doubted it. Her nerves rarely troubled her, but she had felt restless since they went to bed, and her head was aching.

What a wretched day. When Mark lost control of the car she had relived her own accident for a moment, seeing Turner's car shoot towards her, hearing her screams mingle with its engine and the roar of the Skyrider overhead, re-experiencing the agony that had continued till the ambulance men reached her. Today's accident had worried her, too. Mark was a good driver, she'd always felt completely safe with him and the sunlight had not been so very blinding. Was Mark heading for a breakdown, perhaps? Certainly he had been overdoing things recently. He liked the research work at his laboratory – that was part of his life. But there were too many consultations and lectures and hospital visits. Too much brooding as well. If only Mark would forget the loss of their child and adopt one.

'Poor old Mark.' Tania spoke aloud. She had wanted a baby but not craved for one, whereas he . . . She shrugged and took the bottle of aspirins from a shelf. Lucky Mark, too. He'd dropped off as soon as they switched off the lights, while she had tossed and turned with the day's events running unpleasantly through her head.

First the accident, then Ryder's theatrical gesture of drinking the effluent. Had he been worried when Megan forced him to finish the act, or quite certain that the stuff was harmless? Whatever the case, the performance had sickened her. Finally that unpleasant scene in the pub, and the way Willie Price had flushed when he got out to open the car door and saw Ryder's hand gripping Meg's arm and the blood on her sleeve. Willie had obviously imagined that it was his beloved Missus who was injured, and if looks could kill, Daniel Ryder would have dropped to the ground.

What a start to a holiday! Dr Travers and Emrys Hughes and the others were usually courteous men, and Emrys's rudeness had been as unwarranted as Ryder's final outburst. She had felt waves of dislike following her and Mark out into the square, and it would be some time before they set foot in the Leak again.

How hot it was! Tania had made the tea, and she swallowed two aspirins and carried the cup across to the front door. The cottage was warm from the stove, but outside the air was scarcely any cooler. A stifling night, though the sky was clear and the stars a hundred times brighter than she ever saw them in London. There was Arcturus sloping towards Snowdon, there was Venus out to sea, there was a comet. She leaned against the porch with the cup in her hand.

No, not a shooting star; only an aircraft and not a Skyrider this time. There was no hint of modulation in the flat, even drone. She watched it vanish over the hills and smoothed back a lock of hair. Such a hot night, and what odd tricks the moonlight could play! The doorway faced the western flanks of Allt y Cnicht where animals were grazed freely, but the creature moving down the ridge looked bigger than a sheep but too small to be a cow or a bullock. Maybe a goat; a few herds of wild ones still roamed on the mountains.

'Take your shovels to the churchyard, dig old Roberts up and ask him.' The local people resented the archaeologists' activities, that was quite obvious, and Emrys Hughes had been making an insolent joke to annoy Rushton when he said that. The statement had meant nothing, but though the night was so warm, Tania shivered. Mr Justice Roberts was dead and buried, but the cottage was still spoken of as his house. This was the place where he had worked on his books and brooded on the punishment of evil, and through this doorway his murderer had entered. Roberts's body was under six feet of earth, but did his troubled spirit sometimes return home?

Brownies and gnomes, leprechauns, trolls and pixies. Small, stunted creatures which Professor Rushton considered to be the degenerate survivors of a once talented race. As untenable a notion as Tania's own anxieties about Judge Roberts. What nonsense had been talked that evening, she thought, but below in the village the church clock started to strike the hour and she hummed the verse Travers had recited: 'We daren't go a-hunting for fear of little men.'

She stopped humming and looked at the hillside again. Just what was that thing coming towards her along the ridge? It certainly did not move like a sheep or any other four-legged animal. More like an ape trying to walk upright or a bent human figure. That was impossible, of course. There were definitely no apes on Allt y Cnicht, and who would be up there in the small hours of the morning? The creature must be a farm animal, probably a very big ram, and she'd see it clearly when it crossed the next bluff which glinted metallically in the moonlight. Tania laid down her cup and went into the cottage for Mark's binoculars.

Where had the thing gone now? The glasses swept the ridge. More to the right, a little lower? Yes, there it was. She gasped with astonishment because a man was staggering down the Hill of the Knight – a huge man, gleaming like a warrior dressed in silver armour, whose back was so hunched that he appeared deformed. He swung sideways to avoid a boulder; then everything came into perspective, and Tania screamed. The man was not the ghost of some legendary ruler of the mountain, he was not wearing armour and he was not a hunchback. He appeared outsized and deformed because he was bent under a burden. The mangled body of Daniel Ryder was slung over his shoulder and it looked as if a wild beast had savaged him.

Chapter Five

'Let's have him on the sofa.' Mark helped Cedric Bragshaw carry the horribly mutilated body across the room. Half an hour had passed since Tania's scream awakened him and he had rushed out to see Bragshaw stumbling down the mountain under his load. There was no telephone in the cottage; Mark demanded privacy while on holiday, and Tania had gone to break the news to Megan and send for an ambulance.

'Poor devil.' Mark stared down at the thing that had once been a man. He understood that Alpine rocks had caused the earlier injuries to Ryder's face, but now there was hardly any face at all, and Welsh slate and granite had killed him. Apart from a fractured skull, his arms and legs were broken, three of his ribs were staved in, and his clothes were soaked with blood and water.

'The drinks are over there if you could use one.' The Levins had stopped at an off-licence on their way back to the cottage and Mark nodded towards the sideboard.

'Could I use one? That's the understatement of all time.' Bragshaw lurched over and poured out a half-tumbler of neat whisky. He was a powerfully built man who usually moved like a bouncing rubber ball, but the earlier exertion had clearly taxed him. He was breathing heavily and his reddish face had a grey tinge.

'Cheers, old boy.' He lifted the glass and then lowered it hurriedly. 'Good grief, what the hell am I saying? Cheers, indeed, after what's happened!

'Poor old Dan. Not a close pal of mine. I don't think he had any close friends, but I'll be grateful to him till my dying day.' The glass came up again and this time he drank deeply. 'Yes, you saved my bacon, didn't you, Dan?' he said, walking back to the sofa. 'If you hadn't come on the scene, it would have been the bankruptcy court for yours truly.'

Bragshaw stared silently at the corpse for a moment and then looked at Mark. 'Almost ten years ago it was, when Dan and I joined forces. I'd inherited an aircraft assembly business from my father after the war, and was converting military airframes for civilian use. All went well for a while, but when the market became saturated with production models it looked like curtains for us.

'Then Dan approached me with the plans for the Series I Skyrider in his briefcase and an offer to bring us into partnership.' Bragshaw finished his drink. 'Very rough those plans were, but I and my backers could see the possibilities all right, so we raised the capital and went into business. By the time production started we all knew we had a winner. The Skyrider is no oil painting, she's not a racehorse, but there's nothing to beat her for dispatch reliability. After a few years we had three aircraft factories on the go and Dan was building up subsidiary interests – that Linsleat plant and so forth.

'Yes, we made it, didn't we, Dan?' He raised his glass over the sofa. 'Here's to you, old boy, wherever you are now.'

'How did he die, Cedric?' Mark straightened. The corpse was stone-cold and there was nothing to be done for Daniel Ryder. Nothing, except take him back to the cottage hospital he had built for the village, keep him there till Dr Travers, the man who had helped to produce his last fit of anger, certified the cause of death, and then burn or bury him.

'God knows. Obviously he must have slipped, but it's a bloody mystery. Though Dan wasn't wearing proper boots, there was plenty of light and he was one of the most careful mountaineers I've ever known. As I told you, we were business colleagues rather than friends, but we've done some fine climbs together. Dan and I and a chap called Jimmy Mott were the first Englishmen to get up the east wall of the Steinmädchen. Bloody shame he had to be killed on a mouldering slag heap like Allt y Cnicht.

'May I, Mark?' Bragshaw had emptied his tumbler and he went back to the sideboard and refilled it. 'As far as I could make out he must have stumbled on loose scree, created a minor avalanche, and gone over the edge with it. The body was in a stream below a fifty-foot crag and half buried under rubble.'

'Only fifty foot?' Mark mixed himself a drink. Could such a fall have produced those extensive injuries, he wondered. Probably the loose rock that had followed Ryder down was responsible for most of them. 'But just what was he doing up there at that time of night?'

'Working off a temper, Meg said. You and your wife witnessed that scene in the pub when Hughes baited him, didn't you?' Bragshaw's colour had improved and he was breathing easily. 'Well, Dan took that pretty much to heart. There'd been trouble earlier in the year about the hippies he befriended, and he was one hundred per cent behind the archaeologists. He felt that the locals were being deliberately obstructive towards his plans and that Meg was on their side. After running Rushton back to his camp, they quarrelled and he accused her of being a superstitious bigot who was hostile towards Rushton and his team because she was terrified what they might dig up.' Bragshaw lit a cigarette. 'He was right of course. Meg may seem the sophisticated lady of the manor, but she's a peasant under the veneer.

'Anyway, Dan blew his top and made her a challenge. He dared her to prove she was not afraid of the Daran legend by walking over Allt y Cnicht with him then and there. After she refused he punched her one, told Willie Price to stop the car, and stormed off on his own. When Meg last saw him he was striding along the fells as if the devil was at his heels.' Bragshaw lowered himself into an armchair.

'Meg told me all this during dinner and I hardly gave it a

thought. Those two were often at loggerheads, and it seemed a good idea for Dan to calm himself down with a bit of scrambling. Hell's bells, he was an experienced climber and that moon's like a searchlight. He'd be back with his temper cured soon enough, I thought.

'Wasn't till after ten o'clock that I started to get a bit windy and almost eleven when I decided to go and look for him. Meg had said he was wearing shoes and I thought the poor sod might have sprained an ankle. Never once imagined he might have come a real cropper till I found the body.'

'Was Megan worried? Did she offer to go with you?' Mark consulted his watch. Tania must have telephoned the hospital some time ago. Surely the ambulance should be here by now?

'Meg worried? Don't make me laugh, old boy. There was no love lost in that marriage, and Dan had belted her, remember. I could see a bruise through her blouse. Meg said she hoped I'd enjoy the walk but she couldn't care less if he'd broken his neck and she was going to bed.' Bragshaw leaned back in the chair, dragging hard at his cigarette. 'Oh, little Miss Megan will act the bereaved widow efficiently, but she'll be laughing up her sleeve. My guess is that she married Dan to keep the estate intact, and I know there's a clause in their settlement making it over to her in the event of his death. She's got what she wanted all right.'

'Where's that ambulance?' Mark glanced towards the window for a sign of headlights sweeping up the valley. 'If Ryder was lying in a stream, his body was obviously cold when you found it, Cedric, but how long did it take you to get there?'

'About an hour and ten minutes, and of course he was cold as charity.' Even considering that he and Ryder were not close friends, Bragshaw had regained his composure surprisingly rapidly. 'But what does the body temperature matter?

'Ah, I see. You want to pinpoint the time of death.' He had guessed the reason before Mark could answer. Yes, that could be important, because it's one hell of a puzzle why he slipped.

A good, steady climber, who I'd have followed up the Eiger, falling on a scree slope that shouldn't have troubled a one-legged cripple! Meg said he'd had a few drinks, but he wasn't sozzled. You think there's a chance of foul play, Mark? That somebody may have followed him up there and given him a push?'

'Not that. He may have been unpopular, but there's a more innocent explanation.' Mark was considering Ryder's movements. It had been getting on for six when he and Tania reached the manor house, and forty minutes later when they and the others left for the village. Ryder had stormed out of the pub at seven thirty and it would probably have taken him about another half-hour to drive Rushton to his camp, quarrel with Meg and set off up the mountain. Allow him the same time as Bragshaw to reach the place where he died, and what was the rough total? Something in the nature of three hours – which was a long time for any delayed reaction to go unnoticed. All the same, the symptoms observed by the Ministry experts could account for what had happened: cramps, dizziness, nausea and lack of muscular co-ordination. 'I have a strong suspicion that he killed himself.'

'Dan commit suicide?' Bragshaw gave a contemptuous snort. 'You're barking up the wrong tree there, old boy. Dan believed he had a mission in life and chaps with missions don't kill themselves.'

'Sorry, I put it badly. Not actual suicide, but a suicidal gamble was what I meant.' Mark walked back to the body on the sofa. 'Meg refused Ryder's challenge to walk over Allt y Cnicht with him, but you'll remember that she made him a challenge which was accepted.' He sniffed the torn, gaping lips for traces of vomit, but the stream had done its work well and there was no odour to help him. 'Daniel Ryder may have died because he drank that sample of effluent.'

* * *

'Wake up. For God's sake, wake up!' Once again Tania tugged at the handle and heard a bell peal in the distance. 'Surely Megan must have heard that.' She had been ringing the bell and hammering on the door for five minutes at least, and now she stepped back and looked along the rows of unlighted windows.

The manor was not really large by English country-house standards, but around the turn of the century Megan's grand-father had embellished it with features copied from several nobler buildings. A round tower reminiscent of Glamis soared above the roof, parapets were patrolled by stone men-at-arms cribbed from Alnwick Castle, and two heraldic beasts, a gryphon and a dragon, guarded the portico. In daylight the effect was amusing, but under the moon the carved figures looked sinister and the house much bigger than it actually was.

'Oh, come on, Meg.' Tania had returned to the bell-pull, but she was becoming certain nobody would hear her. Megan's bedroom must be out of earshot and there would be nobody else about. Ryder had an aversion to resident servants, and apart from Willie Price who had a bungalow beside the garage, the house was run by daily women.

There was no point in hanging about any longer. Tania gave a final tug and prepared to give up. Her best plan was to drive down to the hospital, and the prospect came as a relief to her. The Ryders might not be a devoted couple, but she didn't relish breaking the news to Megan. She glanced up at the dark windows again and moved back to the car.

Willie Price. His bungalow was out of sight behind the trees, but she'd seen a light when she drove past. Willie was bound to have a key to the house and they could go in and knock Meg up.

Tania turned and walked confidently down the drive. Willie Price was very big, very powerful. Bragshaw was a strong man, but Willie could probably pull him apart with one hand. He looked a bit grotesque with his hanging, expression-less face and long arms, but she felt no anxiety because there was no harm in poor Willie Price. When he'd injured those men after the football match, it had been done in self-defence. Willie wouldn't hurt a fly.

What on earth was he up to, though? Giving a party? She had turned a corner of the house and a blast of music came towards her from a lighted window of the bungalow. A pop song bellowed out by a radio or record player turned to its full volume. Even at this distance the noise was deafening and a series of thuds had joined it. She'd have a job making Willie hear with such a racket going on.

Louder and louder grew the sounds as Tania approached the bungalow, and she smiled as she recalled the saying that a noise can be too loud for one to think. But when she came in line with the window, her expression changed and a hand flew to her mouth.

Not that any cry or scream would have distracted Willie Price, because he was in ecstasy. He was dancing – leaping and capering and swirling around his bedroom – his naked body glistening with sweat and his usually immobile face aglow with excitement.

But it was not only Willie's antics that shocked Tania. On the bed behind him Megan Ryder lay stretched out with her eyes closed. Like Willie she was naked, but the bruises that mottled her shoulders and torso gave a suggestion of clothing.

Chapter Six

'Sorry to have pumped you, my dear, but not to worry. Meg told me how you interrupted her fun and games with Willie Price. Pretended to be ashamed of herself.' A day and a half had passed, and Tania was sitting with Cedric Bragshaw at a table outside the Rose and Leek. Mark was at the hospital and

she had been shopping when Bragshaw met her in the street
and asked her to join him for a drink.

'Masochistic little bitch. I've always suspected that Meg
played around – probably half the lads in the village have had a
go – but I never imagined she took her pleasures savagely. And
with that ape Willie of all people! Cor, stone the crows!' He
guffawed and pulled at his glass tankard. 'You must have had
quite a shock, my dear.'

'That's putting it mildly.' Tania found Bragshaw's humour
irritating because there had been nothing funny about the
scene she witnessed. She could still picture the way Willie's
dance of joy had ended when he saw her standing before the
window. How his body had become rigid and then seemed
to shrink. How he had turned off the record player and then
slunk aside into the shadows like a dog detected in some
major misdeed.

'Please . . . please . . . please, Tania.' Meg Ryder had come
out of the bungalow with a sheet draped around her. There
were tears in her eyes and she spoke in jerks. 'I can't . . . can't
help myself, Tania. Can't help the way I'm made and that was
the first time with Willie . . . never happen again, so don't tell
Dan. Promise me that, Tania. Don't give Dan the chance to
laugh at me.' She had stood swaying on the gravel, and for a
second Tania had felt she was about to go down on her knees
to plead for the promise.

'What . . . what . . . what? Dan dead?' Her mouth had gaped
like an open trap when Tania broke the news. 'No, you're
lying to me. Not true . . . not Dan . . .' Her eyes had closed,
the sheet fell from her shoulders and her bruised body toppled
forward into Tania's arms.

'Do you suppose Ryder knew that Meg played around,
Cedric?' Tania watched a bus draw up beside the post office
and start to take on passengers. There were quite a number
– about twenty men, women and children – and she saw
that most of them were smiling. There seemed to be smiles

everywhere today. She had seen them in the shops and in the streets and at the garage where she had bought petrol and in the bank. Though nobody had mentioned Ryder to her, Tania wondered if his death was responsible for the general good-humour. 'Did he realize that Meg took lovers, and just didn't care, perhaps?'

'I think he must have known, and I've often wondered why he didn't read her the riot act, but this could explain it: Dan was a cold fish but he wanted respect from people. So, when he failed to gain affection by his personality, he tried to buy it.' Bragshaw glanced towards the recreation ground. Children were playing on the swings, their voices shrill in the breeze that had started to blow in from the west. 'Dan had a bitter nature, and when people still did not warm towards him he could become extremely vicious. If Meg had merely been a randy woman, he'd probably have put a stop to her goings on. But masochism is a pretty sad perversion and her craving for humiliation might have amused him. Yes, I think Dan would have got quite a kick out of the thought of her being knocked about by a throw-back like Willie Price.' Bragshaw watched the bus lumber off down the slope towards the main road.

'No, not a pleasant chap, Dan, but Meg's had the last laugh on him. If she hadn't played on his pride and forced him to finish the act and drink that effluent, Dan would still be alive.'

'But there's no evidence that that had anything to do with the accident. Mark suspects that the effluent was toxic; that's why he's gone to see George Travers. But nobody can be certain till the samples sent to London have been analysed.'

'Don't you worry, the analysis will show that Dan swallowed poison, all right.' Bragshaw nodded a greeting as Emrys Hughes passed by on his way to the bar. Like everybody else, the farmer had a grin on his face. 'When I found Dan's body I was too shocked to think clearly and I imagined he must have slipped by accident. But after I'd got him down to the cottage and had a couple of drinks inside me, I started to see that I was wrong. Hell's bells, a climber of his calibre wouldn't fall on such a piffling little traverse, and I began to suspect that someone might have followed him up there and given him a shove.

'But when Mark reminded me about the effluent, the explanation became obvious. Dan was sick, maybe dying, when he fell and he'd only himself to blame. He trusted Graebe and drank poison. Brrr . . . !' Bragshaw grimaced and took another swig of beer.

'Meg will be very pleased that she persuaded him to finish that demonstration of faith, because now she's the lady of the manor in her own right.' He looked towards the big house just visible on the slope. 'I'm sure she did a good fainting act for your benefit, Tania, and she'll put on a public show of mourning, but there'll be no private tears. The estate means everything to little Miss Megan and she has a great pride in family. She once told me that her ancestry went right back to the Celtic tribe that chopped up Daran and his merry men.'

'I thought you didn't believe in that legend, Cedric.' Tania saw a Land Rover cross the square. A woman was driving with with Professor Rushton seated beside her, and she remembered that she and Mark had promised to visit the archaeologists' camp during the afternoon.

'I certainly don't believe any guff about a higher civilization, Tania, but legends must have some foundation. Arthur, Merlin, Robin Hood – they all existed, but in less romantic forms than the story-books tell us. Count Dracula was a real person, you know: a Balkan brigand who made his followers drink human blood because he imagined it was the source of courage. Then, when the vampire bats of South America were discovered, two factual accounts merged into fiction and we finish up with the cinema screen and the good count flying into m'lady's chamber.' Tania's glass was empty and Bragshaw finished his beer and rapped the table for service.

'I suppose Daran was some robber chief who terrorized his neighbours, and they invented rumours of supernatural powers to justify their failure to defeat him. Long afterwards the legends spread and are pushed farther and farther back in time, till you have a superior race and a prehistoric civilization.

'But let's have a refill, my dear? I'll have to get them it seems, because Mrs blasted Ellis is either deaf or bone idle.' He strode off to the bar and Tania studied the hills. Cloud was forming over the more distant summits, but Allt y Cnicht was clear, and from the angle where she was sitting the helmet-shaped peak had a tilted appearance as though the knight was nodding his head over the valley.

'Funny we should have brought up the Daran legend.' Bragshaw's face was thoughtful when he returned. 'That's the sole topic of conversation in the pub. Those superstitious johnnies really do believe that that hill is a source of danger and must not be interfered with. Emrys Hughes was telling his cronies that once Dan's will has been proved, Megan will turn Rushton off her land and put a stop to the digging.

'One can understand Emrys believing the legend, I suppose; he must have had it rammed down his throat since infancy. But for a chap like Doc Travers, an Englishman, to credit such morbid piffle is pretty hard to swallow.

'Yes, old George Travers is a believer.' He followed Tania's stare. 'Used to do a lot of scrambling on Allt y Cnicht once, but no more. He got a bit sozzled one night and told me that he'd studied the effect the mountain had on one of his patients and it had scared the daylights out of him. Said he believed there really might be something a bit uncanny hidden up there and he'd given the north face a wide berth ever since.'

'Judge Roberts was frightened too, Cedric. And why should Rushton and his team be so certain they'll find traces of this early civilization?' The church clock struck the quarter and Tania remembered how she had first seen Bragshaw stumbling along the ridge with Ryder's body. At that moment she herself had almost suspected that some monstrous being might inhabit the mountain.

'Two of the archaeologists called on us yesterday evening. A rather over-charming Frenchman called Georges Destin and a boorish English schoolmistress, whose name I can't remember. They wanted to know if there was a possibility that any of Roberts's papers might be hidden away in the cottage; in the attic or a cupboard, perhaps. When Mark told them that the whole interior had been stripped and rebuilt, the schoolteacher lapsed into gloomy silence, but Destin delivered a lecture on Rushton's lines.'

'I bet he did.' Bragshaw nodded. 'I've met Destin; a little show-off who tries to ape Maurice Chevalier. They'd give their eye-teeth to learn how the judge would have finished his thesis, yet they think he was a nut. Dan once said that old Roberts reckoned there was some kind of evil shrine on the mountain, and believed that Daran was a Satanic priest, who not only overawed his enemies by witchcraft but had the power to blight crops and spread disease.

'Pah ! Belief . . . faith . . . visions of immortality. They make me want to vomit.' Bragshaw was obviously a fervid atheist. 'The disease yarn presumably started because Allt y Cnicht has always been lousy with adders and there must have been quite a few bites over the years. What a profitable industry the supernatural is! Think of all the faith-healers, fortune-tellers and fake Indian gurus who must be grinning at their bank accounts right now. People long for evidence of a spirit world, and when they're persuaded it exists, the poor dupes get the wind up and picture ghouls and vampires and three-headed devils howling on the ruined church steeple.'

'What'll happen to those poor kids?' Tania had once been an atheist herself, but since living in England, she had developed a keen interest in the occult and Bragshaw's remarks infuriated her. She changed the subject and pointed at a man on the opposite pavement. He wore ragged jeans, his hair and beard were uncombed and his face was ashen. Though very young, almost a boy, he was walking slowly and falteringly as though the slope was too steep for him. 'I suppose Megan will be asked to get rid of them as well as the archaeologists?'

'Probably. The Treflys locals are a puritanical lot who don't approve of eccentric strangers. Can't blame 'em where those young layabouts are concerned.' Bragshaw raised the tankard, obviously indifferent to the fate of Ryder's protégés, and then his body stiffened and he held the glass suspended before his lips.

'No, they don't like a certain type of visitor, do they? And, as I said, people can get very, very frightened of the occult . . . obsessed with it. So I'm wondering, Tania, just wondering whether . . .' He put down the glass with a click.

'I don't think you and Mark have ever been to the top of Allt y Cnicht, so what about an expedition tomorrow? We'll go by way of the crag where Dan fell.' He cupped his chin in his hand and leaned across the table like a grotesque parody of Rodin's 'Thinker'. 'If that effluent was poisoned, well and good. If not, I intend to take a very close look at the scene of that so-called accident.'

*   *   *

'This is all a bit beyond me, gentlemen.' Police Constable Ivor Johns lowered his notebook. He and Mark were facing each other in the matron's office at the cottage hospital, and behind her desk Dr Travers was busily doodling on a blotter.

'Till you mentioned this stuff Mr Ryder drank, there didn't seem to be any mystery at all about his death, sir . . . Sir Marcus.' Johns hesitated over the title. As a policeman he had to pay lip service to the Establishment, but he hailed from the Rhondda and in private was a staunch socialist fuelled by memories of strikes and lockouts and hunger marches inherited from his parents.

'Just a plain accident was what I thought. Mr Ryder slipped over a cliff and brought about a ton of loose rock down on top of him. Everybody knows what death-traps there are on that mountain. Warning notices the County Council have put up, and that's why the Mine Commissioners built their dynamite store under the north face. No kids'll go exploring round there in a hurry, and it's my belief that those old tales were made up for that very reason. Scare stories to keep the children away from Allt y Cnicht and out of danger, and they're much better warnings than any Council notices, eh, Doctor?' He looked at the desk for support, but Travers seemed engrossed with his doodles.

'A sad and tragic loss, Sir Marcus, but if a man with drink inside him goes scrambling up a treacherous mountain at night, what can one expect?' Though Johns spoke piously, he did not regard Ryder's death as at all tragic. He had disliked Ryder personally and the man had been a capitalist, an exploiter of labour, a grinder of the faces of the poor.

'Yes, a good deal of drink.' The policeman consulted his notes. 'Mrs Ryder informed me that her husband had had three large pink gins at the house and followed them with three pints of bitter at the Rose and Leek. Not enough to make him drunk, perhaps, but quite enough to slow down his reactions and account for the fall. And now you're telling me he was poisoned, Sir Marcus.'

'I have said no such thing.' Mark was trying to keep his temper. 'I merely pointed out that Mr Ryder also drank a glass of chemical effluent. The stuff may have been harmless, as he obviously believed himself, but we can't be sure till the other samples have been analysed.' Mark looked at the telephone. He had called Kirk earlier, and the general had promised to ring him at the hospital as soon as he had information. At any moment he might know whether his suspicions were justified. 'The analyst's report is long overdue; God knows when it will be ready, and while we're waiting I would like to examine Mr Ryder's body and carry out certain tests. That is surely a matter between myself and Dr Travers, Constable, and I must

say that I am rather at a loss to know why you are present at
our meeting.'

'Because I asked him to be present, Mark.' Travers pushed
aside the blotter. 'Constable Johns is our local police officer
and I am the police doctor. If there is a suggestion of negligence on my part, he should know about it.

'No, let me have my say, please.' He raised his hand as Mark
tried to break in. 'At your request, Ryder's body has been examined and the necessary tests have been made; by Dr Glynn-
Jones and myself.' George Travers spoke quietly, but there
was a hint of hostility in his tone. 'None of the seven classified
poison groups were present in the organs and because of the
time factor we did not expect to find any. A micro-organism
such as salmonella or ptomaine would not have revealed itself
for a good twelve hours, while a corrosive poison would have
acted before Ryder even reached the Rose and Leek.

'We are not Nobel Prize winners, or London specialists,
Mark, but Glynn-Jones and I have carried out a great many
autopsies, and I have held the post of police surgeon for a very
long time. Our examination of Ryder's body was thorough in
the extreme, but apparently you are not satisfied and wish to
carry out your own autopsy, and I would like to know why. Do
you doubt our professional abilities?'

'Don't be so damn sensitive, George.' Mark's irritation
was on the boil, though he could sympathize with Travers's
feelings. The old man had practised locally for thirty-five years
and where Treflys was concerned he and his assistant, Glynn-
Jones, were the medical profession. He had no competitors,
he lorded it over the hospital and the Public Health Department, and, as he had said, he was the police doctor. If he had
blundered and it was proved that there was poison in Ryder's
body, his pride and reputation would suffer a severe blow.

'All I want is the opportunity to join you in a second examination, George.' He frowned at Johns, realizing why the constable had been asked to the interview. Travers knew that if

they had been alone Mark would have harried him tooth and nail, tested his forensic knowledge, fired questions to see how well he had kept up with modern research and badgered him into agreement. But professional etiquette ensured that, with a layman present, he could only plead.

'I am not criticizing you or Glynn-Jones at all, George, but surely my request is not unreasonable, and I do have some slight advantages over you. The effluent that Ryder drank came from Linsleat and I have studied the reports on the wildlife that was infected there earlier this year. I was also consulted about the cases of food poisoning at the Mansion House and this is why I am making my request. People fell ill because they ate Linsleat oysters, but the oysters themselves were not diseased in the accepted sense of the word. They had an abnormal iodine content; but none of the seven recognized poison groups you mentioned were found to account for it. Nobody knows what the causative agent was.'

'Heh, heh, heh! An undetected poison.' Travers cackled like an old woman. 'Is that what sent Daniel Ryder to his eternal rest? Some secret preparation concocted by African witch-doctors or a mysterious tribe up the Amazon. This is most serious, Constable Johns. Perhaps you should summon Scotland Yard to your aid.'

'Laugh as much as you like, George, but unidentified poisons do exist.' Mark's voice rose with his temper and became foreign and strident: Israel wailing at Aryan stupidity. 'Poisons that should be easy to recognize, but go undetected because doctors haven't their wits about them.'

'Naughty, naughty, Mark.' The old man leaned back in his chair. 'That was an insolent crack, which I would have resented from most people. However, you did me a favour by helping to run the practice while I was laid up, and no hard feelings.

'All the same, I'm very sorry but there'll be no second autopsy without a magistrate's order.' The telephone rang and he reached out. 'Excuse me while I answer this.

'Ah, the call's for you, Mark. Let's hope it's the information we need to clear the air.'

'That you, Charles?' Mark had almost snatched the instrument from Travers. 'Have those results come through yet?'

'They have, Mark, and high time, too.' The line was bad and Kirk raised his voice. 'Apparently Professor Goater was tied up with other business but insisted on doing the analysis himself, vainglorious ass. However, this is what he found. The effluent was broken down into the following quantities: 1.5 per cent cellulose nitrate, 0.3 per cent casein, 0.8 per cent –'

'And nothing else, Charles?' Mark had jotted down the chemical composition. 'What a bloody shame, but it's quite conclusive, I'm afraid. Anyway, thanks for letting me know, and goodbye for the present.' He replaced the receiver and looked at Travers.

'That's that, George, and I'm sorry if I sounded rude just now – though I admit that I meant to be rude. The effluent Ryder drank was one of several sealed samples and the others contained nothing which could have harmed him.' He handed Travers the formula and smiled apologetically at Johns.

'Accidental death, as you both thought, gentlemen, and I regret having wasted your time.' Mark picked up his hat. D.R. Products was in the clear and, whatever the cause of the Linsleat epidemics, they were no longer his concern. He turned to leave, determined to put the matter out of his mind and enjoy what was left of his holiday. But he was to be disappointed. At about the same moment that his hand reached the doorknob, another hand had delivered an order that would set him hard at work.

* * *

'We're finally ready to fish, are we, Mr Magill? I'm delighted to hear it, but no congratulations are due to you.' Captain James

Clegg of the Larne trawler *Loyal Apprentice* raised his hand and rang the engine telegraph for towing speed.

'Do you know how long it took you to get the nets out, Mister?' Clegg would have liked to vent his annoyance with a string of curses, but he was a strict Presbyterian who regarded profanity as an abomination to God. 'Exactly eight minutes too long, and you'll have to do better than that if you want to keep your berth on this ship. Those fellers are idlers, Mister. They've got to be driven till they crack.'

He scowled at his mate and stumped out on to the flying-bridge, feeling a deep sympathy for Captain Bligh, while he watched the hands at work on deck. The voyage had started well enough, the early catches were promising, but yesterday morning the trawl had been fouled by a wartime wreck and he had had to put into Londonderry for repairs. Like a fool, he had granted shore-leave to the men not actually needed for the operations, and many of them had returned sodden and half-useless from the dockside bars. Worse than that, his cook had been involved in a street fight with a gang of Catholics and was under arrest for causing 'Grievous Bodily Harm'. Clegg couldn't blame the man – he himself hated papists body and soul and mind – but he didn't relish a spell of the galley boy's cooking.

'A grand day though, skipper.' Magill crossed over to him as the deck shuddered and the diesel revolutions built up to drag the eighty-foot trawl forward. He was a young man, but he had no fears that his captain would carry out any threat to replace him. Old Clegg might glory in the nickname of 'Gadfly', but however much he barked, he rarely bit and his crew regarded him with affection and respect. 'Aye, a fine man, Jimmy Clegg,' they said. 'Past president of an Orange lodge and one of the best – the very best.' Once their hangovers had worn off, they'd work for him till they dropped.

And not only out of emotional regard, of course. The *Apprentice* was a lucky ship on the whole, and it was a rare occasion when they returned to port without full holds. Clegg was a conservative who still used an outdated otter-trawl, but he had an uncanny instinct for picking the right fishing grounds. At the moment, they were crossing Mulligan's Bank, eleven miles north-north-east of the Linsleat estuary, and Magill had no doubt that the catch would be heavy.

'A nice day at the moment, Mister, but this weather won't last, whatever the forecasters say. I can smell fog coming in and there'll be a wind behind it.' Clegg picked up his binoculars and studied the horizons. The mainland hills were clear, but there was a hint of cloud beyond Rathlin Island.

Linsleat! That'll be the next place where the murdering swine will make trouble; another Derry, another Belfast, he thought, as his glasses swept the mouth of the estuary. And they'd started already; though the government denied it, every sane man knew that. Poisoning the fish with chemicals – a foul trick to deprive honest men of their livelihoods; but what could you expect from *them*? From papists who knelt before idols and ran arms and explosives in from the south to kill women and children. Clegg's daughter had been injured in a bomb explosion in Belfast and she would never walk again.

And the arms didn't only come in from the south, either; he was quite convinced of that. There had been a fleet of Russian trawlers off the coast all the summer, and on two occasions he'd seen a Republican boat alongside one of them. The Russians would be only too happy to supply the murderers with weapons.

'One of Thracian Oil's, Mister.' He turned the glasses away from Linsleat and trained them on a big tanker coming towards the *Apprentice* on a parallel course. She was so low in the water that her catwalks were awash, and the stern and central superstructures looked as if they belonged to two separate vessels.

'Oh, no, don't tell me that we're going to have company again.' His face flushed beneath its deep tan and he lowered the binoculars and handed them to Magill. 'Have a look, lad, your eyes are better than mine.'

'Afraid you're right, skipper.' The mate studied a fishing vessel that was far astern of them but coming up fast. 'That's the *Tyrconnell* or I'm a Dutchman. We've seen too much of her for me to be wrong.'

'We certainly *have* seen too much of her.' Clegg's fury was mounting. Several times in the past the *Tyrconnell,* a Donegal trawler, had dogged the *Apprentice,* and he was certain that her master, Tim O'Ryan, intended to cash in on his knack of picking the best fishing grounds. Not only was the man a thief who preyed on his skill, but the very name of his boat offended Clegg. Tyrconnell, the papist who had tried to starve out Derry in 1688.

'Poaching thieves hoping to muscle in on our catch, and judging by the feel of the trawl, there's a fine shoal beneath us.' He took the glasses again. The *Tyrconnell* was not a good sea boat – she was pitching violently – but her engines were impressive and she was closing on the *Apprentice* rapidly.

'You know, lad, I'm getting a bit tired of showing Mr O'Ryan where to fish, and it's time to put a stop to it. Tell the blighters that I'll run across their trawl if they come within half a mile of us.'

'Aye, aye, skipper,' Magill picked up an Aldis lamp and flashed out the message. He repeated it three times and then frowned at Clegg. 'No reply, sir, and the funny thing is that I can't see anybody on the bridge.'

'Playing possum in the wheelhouse, are they? Likes a little joke, does Mr O'Ryan. Well, I'm going to be the joker today.' He grinned at the concern on Magill's face. 'Don't worry, lad, I won't foul the nets and earn myself a rocket from the owners, but I'll give those thieving Turks a lesson they won't forget. I'll scare the daylights out of them.

'Cameron.' He turned to the quartermaster at the wheel. 'You'll have heard what me and Mr Magill were planning, so keep on your toes. Apparently our Republican friends are too ignorant to read a Morse lamp and we must educate them. When I give the word, swing right across their bows.' Clegg lit a cigarette and watched the approach of the *Tyrconnell*. His anger had changed to glee at the thought of O'Ryan's horrified surprise when the *Apprentice* came lumbering towards him.

They don't believe we'll do it, he thought, but as Magill had said, it was strange that he could see nobody on the bridge. Also curious why the Turks should be flogging their ship so hard. The *Tyrconnell*'s wake was boiling like a destroyer's and he could hear the beat of her engine. Well, in a moment or two O'Ryan would be bellowing at his helmsman and ringing his telegraph to reduce speed.

'Get ready, Cameron.' He watched the bow wave pluming towards the *Apprentice* and judged the distance. Not too close; there must be no risk of a collision, and he had to allow O'Ryan ample room to swing aside. But close enough to give him a shock and teach him manners.

'Here we go. Hard a-starboard, Cameron.' He raised a loud-hailer as the wheel was swung over and the rudder started to bite.

'Hop it, O'Ryan. Get out of the way, you I.R.A. pope-lover.' Clegg shouted gleefully from the lurching deck and with the trawl acting as a hinge the ship spun round into the *Tyrconnell*'s seaway. 'Clear off or I'll ram you.' Yard by yard the two vessels converged, but there was still no sign of life on the Donegal boat. The spray still plumed at her bows, she made no move to alter course, and all at once Clegg realized that she would not turn aside.

'Over to port, Cameron,' he screamed, seeing death hurtling down on him, and then he lifted the loud-hailer again. 'Pull away from us, O'Ryan. Come to your senses, man, and pull over.' He braced himself against a stanchion, his voice competing with the roar of the ships' engines, but still the *Tyrconnell* came on.

When he was a boy, James Clegg had solemnly promised his parents that he would never use obscenities or take the Lord's name in vain. A hard thing for a trawler skipper to do, but he had kept the promise for forty-three years. It was rather sad that his last words should be 'Bugger off, O'Ryan. For Christ's sake, sod off, you bloody Catholic bastard.'

Chapter Seven

'Men of Harlech, lie ye dreaming? See ye not their falcons gleaming?' Mark had heard several versions of the song, and he improvised on one of them as he toiled up the west side of Allt y Cnicht. 'While their pennons gaily streaming flutter in the breeze.

'From the rocks rebounding ... hear the war cry sounding ...' If any pennons were available they would be streaming today, he thought as he hummed. The wind that had sprung up during the night had increased to near gale force, and little scudding clouds were hurrying across the sky. Most of the time the three climbers were in sunlight with gusts tugging at their clothes, but now and again some corner of the mountain would deflect the wind, and swirling mist surrounded them.

That fellow certainly believes in keeping up the pressure. Mark was some distance behind Bragshaw and Tania, and he scowled at their boots pounding remorselessly along the ever-steepening slope. In places the arête was only a couple of yards wide, there was a near-vertical drop on either side, and the rocks were loose and slippery. But Cedric Bragshaw strode on as though he were hurrying to catch a train, and it galled Mark that Tania appeared to be having no difficulty in keeping up with him. But then she was a young woman who played golf twice a week to keep herself fit. This first bout of violent exercise was no pleasure for a middle-aged scientist who spent half his life at a laboratory bench.

Still, he should get his second wind in time and the view was almost worth the effort. The ridge was swinging to the left to reveal the helmeted summit high above them, while the northern cliffs plunged down towards the lane leading to the dynamite store. Ignoring his companions, Mark halted and trained his binoculars at three squat buildings surrounded by barbed wire and warning notices, which reminded him of Belsen.

'Arbeit macht frei'; he muttered the Nazi slogan to himself, thinking of the wired compounds of his youth, and then he pushed the images aside and studied the buildings. They had massively thick walls and light corrugated-iron roofs with little upward resistance. Should the dynamite be accidentally detonated, its force would be contained by the walls and released harmlessly into the sky. A very necessary precaution: Emrys Hughes had once told him that enough explosives were stored there to destroy a fair-sized town.

Always hard at work. The glasses moved along the base of the cliff, and a cluster of antlike figures came into view: the archaeologists, busily searching for the traces of civilization. He and Tania had visited the site of their operations yesterday and, though the survey was obviously in its early stages, Rushton had shown them fragments of bronze and broken crockery and a slate slab with curious carvings which he believed to be pre-Gaelic in origin.

Though material progress was not all that spectacular, Mark had been impressed by the team itself. As Rushton had said, they were a diverse gathering ranging from students to retired people; besides the Frenchman and the schoolmistress who had called at the cottage, they had been introduced to a Dutch lawyer, an Italian dentist and the widow of a Swiss garage proprietor. Apparently the group had been brought together by an article published by Rushton in an archaeological journal – and they were all full of enthusiasm, all convinced that their labours would be rewarded. The young hacking and shovelling, and the elderly industriously sorting through the material that was dislodged.

'Hurry up, old boy. No loitering.' Bragshaw's voice bellowed out from a pocket of mist. 'This bloody fog is going to get thicker before long.'

'I'm coming.' Mark lowered the glasses and toiled on. At the foot of the climb they had passed a notice warning visitors against loose rock, bogs, adders and other hazards, and he saw how justified the warnings were. The ridge was joining the main massif, and the plateau ahead made him think of a moon landscape. The ground was riddled with deep cracks and fissures and all over it jagged boulders reared upright like tombstones. The Treflys farmers might be superstitious; but, as they said, the mountain was a monstrosity and they had good practical reasons for keeping their animals away from this part of it.

'Not far to go now.' Bragshaw and Tania were waiting for him at the edge of the plateau, and Bragshaw pointed to the crag forming the first steps of the climb to the summit. 'That's where Dan Ryder was killed, and we'll stay close together over this bit. It's pretty treacherous, and if Dan had fallen here, I wouldn't have any doubts that it was an accident. I had one hell of a job carrying his body across. Had to drag the poor bastard at times.

'What's the matter, my dear? Feeling a bit windy?' Tania was staring back down the ridge and Bragshaw fingered a coil of nylon line slung over his shoulder. 'Should I put you on the rope?'

'No, I don't think I'll need any help and I'm not nervous. Not of the climb, that is, but a few minutes ago I had a feeling that we weren't alone – that somebody was following us.' She laid her hand on Mark's arm. 'Did you hear anything, darling? I've had the same sensation again, just now.'

'No, all I can hear is the wind and that contraption.' He nodded towards a Skyrider circling the far side of the valley.

'Noisy bastards, aren't they? She'll be carrying out her low-flying trials. Our Llancir factory is only about twenty miles away.' The engine notes echoed from the crags around them and Bragshaw scowled. 'Ryder's sick symphony, the fitters call that. On the test bed, the noise burns into your brain like a red-hot needle.'

'You disapprove of it, Cedric? Surely as a director you were partly responsible?'

'Not on your Nellie, old boy. The board and the design staff thought that a resonated exhaust system was a waste of time and money, but Dan was adamant, and as usual he overruled us. He considered aircraft annoyance could be lessened by varying the exhaust flow to produce modulated sound frequencies ... consulted acoustics experts to back him up and was as pleased as punch when he worked out the system, but in my opinion it was a waste of time. Those engines are as irritating as any others.

'Mind how you go, now. As I said, this bit's rather tricky.' The plane was out of sight and Bragshaw started off across the plateau. 'But though Dan's end-product was a wash-out, the technique he used was pretty brilliant and you've got to hand it to him. The accepted modern method of noise reduction is to fit fan jets, but Dan's is much more unorthodox. The Rydercraft engines have vented rotor-blades, and the exhaust passes through three grills set at varying angles. This creates the frequency changes and Bob's your uncle.' Bragshaw moved slowly across the rough ground and he planted his feet very carefully.

'Strange how a brilliant technician could get a bee in his bonnet. Dan must have put as much work into those exhaust modulations as anything else he designed. Tape-recordings of the aircraft operating at different speeds and altitudes were made, and he kept changing the angles of the grills till he was satisfied.' He paused and helped Tania across a crevasse.

'Poor old Dan. The sound problem became an obsession

with him, and after the new engines were first fitted to the Model III Skyrider, he had questionnaires prepared – to test public reaction. They were sent to every country where the planes were in service and he went through each completed form personally.

'Like a ruddy cats' chorus, isn't it?' The Skyrider was above them again, swinging round to return to her base, and Bragshaw shook his head. 'A complete piece of nonsense, but Dan was a martinet who'd never take no for an answer. He put another pet scheme into operation recently which is just as useless. We've always used Hailey-Kerr airspeed indicators and they give complete satisfaction. But a few months ago Dan insisted we cancel our order with Hailey's, and the new airframes are to be fitted with a Russian model which is no more efficient and a damn sight more expensive. God knows what his reason was.'

'There must have been a reason, though.' Tania was working her way between a cluster of rocks. The sun was clear again, but – for the third time – she had had an uneasy feeling that they were being followed. 'Ryder was a businessman. He wouldn't throw money away if the Soviet instruments weren't superior.'

'Presumably he considered they were better, but he never even bothered to try to convince me. Just told the board to place the order.' The slope was steepening towards the crags, but the terrain had become less broken and Bragshaw increased his pace. 'One of my fellow directors suggested he might have had a rake-off from the Bolshies, but I soon told him where he got off. Dan might be eccentric, but we'd done a lot of climbs together and I'm sure he was as honest as they come. And I'm also quite sure that the poor devil didn't fall over that crag accidentally.' They were below the cliffs now and Bragshaw turned left up a rough staircase of boulders.

'Just a little bit of scrambling and you'll see what I mean.' He led the way forward, moving easily over the rocks, and then waited for Tania and Mark to reach him. 'Well, that's it, and what do you think? Neither of you are climbers, but would you have any difficulty getting across there?'

'You mean this is where Ryder fell?' Mark stood beside him, breathing heavily. Though the incline had been steep, he quite understood why Bragshaw should be suspicious. The crag was rather like a two-tiered wedding cake, with its levels divided by a stretch of scree. But though the scree was obviously loose, it sloped towards the lower cliff at an easy angle of about thirty degrees.

'Yes, Mark, this is the place where the man who led me up the Steinmädchen is supposed to have lost his balance.' Bragshaw strolled nonchalantly to the edge and Mark and Tania had no qualms about following him. 'And it happened in bright moonlight, remember. Better visibility than we've got at the moment.' A cloud was under the sun and, as he had predicted, the mist was thickening, swirling in spirals across the plateau; soon they might be in semi-darkness.

'Lost his balance, my foot! If we can rule out that stuff he drank, there are only two explanations. Either Dan was startled by something, or somebody pushed him.'

'I take your point.' Mark craned forward. Fifty feet below them lay the stream into which Daniel Ryder had fallen. Loose rocks were strewn along its banks and some of them must have gone over the edge with Ryder and caused his terrible injuries. Till a moment ago Mark had ruled out foul play, but his opinion was faltering. Ryder was an experienced climber and the effluent contained nothing to account for vertigo. An ordinary mishap did seem unlikely, but all the same ... He drew back, remembering Ryder's broken nose and paralysed cheek.

'There's another possibility, Cedric. Maybe Ryder was accident prone. He had a fall in the French Alps once, and I wonder how many other climbing accidents he might have been involved in.'

'Don't talk bilge.' Bragshaw snorted his contempt. 'First *I've* heard of Dan falling off anything. He was as steady as a chamois. Oh, you think he smashed his face while he was climbing? You've got it wrong, old boy; that was quite a different kind of accident.'

'Keep quiet, both of you.' Tania hissed the warning because she now knew that she had not been imagining things. They were being followed, and from somewhere below the crags she could hear footsteps and the occasional rattle of scree. Mark and Bragshaw also heard it, and the three of them stood staring around them and trying to determine from where the sounds came. Then a sudden gust cleared the mist and Mark pointed down the route they had come.

Crawling towards them, looking grotesque and ungainly as he negotiated the slope on his hands and knees, came Willie Price.

* * *

'Mrs Ryder just said you were to come after us, Willie?' They were on the way back, roped together and moving cautiously down the ridge. The wind had dropped, fine rain had joined the mist, and visibility was down to a few yards. 'She said it was urgent that we came back, but she didn't tell you why?'

'Missus just said I was to find you, Sir Marcus.' Bragshaw was bringing up the rear and Price was linked between Mark and Tania, lumbering along on the rope like a performing bear. ' "You get up there and fetch 'em, Willie." That's what she said. "Quick about it, now. This is urgent and I want 'em down here right away."

'I didn't want to go, did I? Don't like being on old Allt y Cnicht by myself. Only done it once before, and scared I was in the fog – right glad when I found you. But I had no choice, had I? Must do what Missus says.'

'Urgent? That's all she told you?' Tania had noted the

respect in Willie's voice as he used the word 'Missus'. Yet only a short time ago she had seen him capering before Megan Ryder's bruised body.

'That's right, mum.' Price stumbled and the rope jarred against Mark. But the worst of the journey was over, they were almost below the cloud, and the valley was coming into sight. 'I was washing the car when Missus called me. Said I was to cycle up to Mr Roberts's cottage and fetch Sir Marcus. But I told her it was no good, because I'd seen the three of you setting off up the mountain. Right angry Missus got when she heard that. Went red in the face, she did, and you can't blame her. Natural she should be cross.'

'What the hell do you mean, Price?' Bragshaw had been frustrated at having to return before they made a full inspection at the scene of Ryder's accident, and it was his turn to sound angry. 'Why should your mistress be annoyed because we came up here?'

'Don't rightly know, sir.' Though Price's back was towards him, Mark could see embarrassment in every movement of his huge body. 'Maybe I was wrong and she was just worried. Thought you might have a fall like her husband did.'

'All right, let's stop and get the rope off. The mist's cleared and there's no need for it.' Bragshaw brought them to a halt. 'Now, listen to me, Willie Price. You may be a fool, but you can understand plain English. You said Mrs Ryder was angry, and anger and worry are two different things.' He spoke like a schoolmaster addressing a troublesome pupil. 'Why was she angry and why do you think it was natural for her to be angry?'

'Maybe she thought you should have asked permission before walking about on her land, sir.' Price fumbled clumsily to undo the knotted rope, and he clearly regretted mentioning Meg's emotions. 'I mean Allt y Cnicht is her land, ain't it? Missus owns everything now that he's dead.'

'He? You mean *Mister* Ryder, I presume.' They were all untied and Bragshaw coiled up the nylon line. 'God, you really are a fool, Price. I happen to be a guest at the manor, and do you honestly think Mrs Ryder would object to her friends going where they liked?'

'Dunno, sir – not my place to say. But I heard talk in the village that things are going to be different from now on. She'll get rid of that bunch for one thing, and high time too.' He stood looking towards the archaeologists' camp. 'Ryder should never have let 'em come here. Never have let 'em start their blasted diggings. Terrible trouble they could bring to the valley, real bad trouble.'

'Come on and let's get going. I'm tired of listening to gibberish.' Bragshaw threw the rope over his shoulder and started forward; but Willie Price had an axe to grind and he shouted after him.

'And they hippies as well, Mr Bragshaw. She'll send 'em packing right enough. Smokin' pot, stickin' needles into themselves and all sleepin' together like bleeding animals. Why did Ryder invite the bastards here, that's what we'd like to know. Some of us think it was him that was giving the stuff to 'em.'

'What? What's that?' Bragshaw swung round in a fury. 'People have been suggesting that Mr Ryder was supplying those kids with drugs? Which people, Price? I want their names, so out with them.' He had walked back with a scowl on his face, but as he did so, something that looked like a green necktie whipped around his ankle, the scowl became an agonized grimace and he lurched sideways. He was almost over the lip of the precipice when Mark dragged him back.

★   ★   ★

'That's all right, then.' Mark put down the telephone and turned to Tania and Megan Ryder. Willie Price had made light work of bringing Bragshaw down to the manor house and he was in bed, cursing his luck but quite comfortable.

'Though I think I sucked out most of the poison, Bangor hospital are sending over some serum for good measure and the man's as strong as a horse. He'll have to rest up for a bit, but adder bites are rarely serious and there's nothing to worry about.'

'I imagine Cedric's temper will be the worst sufferer. He intended to go to the Llancir factory tomorrow.' Megan walked over to a cocktail cabinet. Bragshaw had said that she would play the bereaved widow efficiently, and Willie Price thought she was angry. They both appeared to be wrong. Though Meg wore a black costume, it was short and stylish with little suggestion of mourning and Mark had never seen her look so radiant.

'Poor dear Cedric. He always scoffed when I told him that Allt y Cnicht was a good place to keep away from. Poor Daniel, as well.' She added her husband's name almost as an afterthought. 'Just two more victims of our unlucky mountain.

'What about a drink? You've certainly earned one by saving Cedric's life, Mark. He told me he almost went over the edge when the snake bit him. "If that fellow hadn't grabbed me, I'd have gone for a Burton," was the way he naturally described it.' Meg drew out three glasses and then turned with an irritated frown.

'But how stupid I am. Thinking about Cedric made me quite forget why I sent Willie Price after you.' She lifted her handbag from a chair and Tania saw that a bruise on her left arm was still purple. 'Miss Glynn at the post office rang and asked if I could pass on a telegram to you, Mark. I didn't want to spoil your expedition, but the contents sounded a bit life-and-deathish.' She handed him a sheet of notepaper. 'I wrote it down word for word.'

'Thank you, Meg.' Her writing was small and cramped and he held the paper towards the light. The telegram had been sent from London and its message read, 'Imperative that you contact me immediately and return here without delay.' The signature was Kirk's and another sentence followed it: 'You may be on holiday, but why aren't you on the blasted phone?'

Chapter Eight

'My dear friend, you don't have to remind me of our relationship. We are comrades who must trust each other implicitly, and that is why I find your anxiety rather irritating.' The man was speaking into a telephone and his foreign accent rasped the words as though he was an army officer delivering orders. He enjoyed giving orders – he liked to think of himself as an officer, a man of authority, a captain of industry – he liked having people obey him.

'The inspectors expressed themselves satisfied with D.R.'s former disposal arrangements, analysis has shown the effluent to be non-toxic, so what the hell are you worrying about?' Though the man was middle-aged, his face was as unlined as a boy's and his thinning hair dyed bright auburn. From the neck up he looked youthful, but the rest of his body betrayed his years. Apart from his belly, which bulged obscenely beneath a newspaper spread out before him, it was bent and scraggy and ill. He lay on a sofa, and he reeked of scent and moral corruption.

'Nothing can go wrong here, but your news is disturbing, to say the least. I presume it is quite definite that our friend passed on accidentally?' He stared out through a window while he listened, watching the Linsleat estuary with hard, emotionless eyes. The new town appeared almost Mediterranean in the sunlight, birds wheeled over the island, and a motorized barge was rounding the headland: the hopper hired by D.R. Products to carry their waste materials out to sea. Very soon it could return to its owners because the ban would have been lifted and another source of pollution investigated.

A peaceful scene, but how long would it last, he wondered, glancing at his newspaper. The loss of the *Loyal Apprentice* and the *Tyrconnell* filled most of the front page and the death roll was impressive. The two skippers, one Catholic, one Protestant, appeared to have staged a naval battle, and before long land battles would follow. Soon the captains' co-religionists would call for revenge and the gangs come out in Linsleat. That did not worry the man in the slightest. What did it matter if a few houses burned and a few brainless skulls got broken. He'd seen a lot of violence in his time and most of it had amused him.

'A pure accident, then. How sad, but nothing is altered and what does the body matter?' An aircraft was climbing into the sky and the man looked at his watch. Flight 205 from Belfast to Boston and dead on time. Only air and water between it and the Nantucket light. The distant drone stirred his memories of violence and he recalled a song he had so often chanted in his youth. He had trained himself to think bilingually and the words ran through his head in English and German. 'The banners high, the ranks are closed together . . . *S.A. marschiert in ruhig festen Schritt . . .*'

'Now, what news of your progress?' He frowned at his caller's answer. 'I see. You are quite sure about the general location, but it will take time to find the actual place itself. That is understandable – there are so many possibilities – but please do your utmost. Please be as quick as you can, because I would so much like to have the business completed before this body rots.' He slid a hand under the newspaper and kneaded his swollen stomach.

'Excuse me one moment.' There had been a knock on the door and he nodded formally to his secretary as she entered the room. Then, when he looked away from her, his glance fell on the paper; the look of indifference left his eyes and they seemed to draw far back into his skull. 'Shut up and don't interrupt me.' He snapped into the telephone because the stop-press announcement he had just noticed held his thoughts like a magnet: TRAWLER DISASTER – BOS'N'S STATE-MENT.

'Please listen carefully.' He resumed the conversation in a foreign language. 'I may have been over-confident and there could have been a slip-up after all. I don't think this is so, but we can't wait any longer. Time could be against us and you will have to use extreme methods to find him. Run any risks, exert any pressure available, but find him – you must find him quickly.' Though he used his native tongue, he spoke slowly and haltingly, faltering over each phrase as if the words were unfamiliar to him, and his concentration made him quite oblivious of his secretary, who sat arranging her desk. There was no possibility that she could understand the language he was speaking. Very few people could.

*   *   *

It had been a slow, wearisome journey from Treflys and it was a foul evening in London. Mark nosed his car through the West End traffic and the rain that had been falling in sheets since he left the motorway, and he felt glad that he had per-suaded Tania to remain in Wales. She had appeared fitter than himself during the climb up Allt y Cnicht, but was obviously very tired by the time he had spoken to Kirk on the telephone, and it would have been ridiculous for her to have joined him.

'Yes, my dear boy, I may certainly be bringing you back on a fool's errand,' Kirk had said. 'But in my opinion Goater is an incompetent fool and we need your wisdom and expertise most urgently. You see there could be a connection between the Linsleat business and the loss of those fishing boats.

'What? You haven't heard about the trawlers? You really do withdraw from the world, Mark.' Mark could almost picture Kirk's raised eyebrows. 'Listen to your car radio on the way and please get to Central Laboratories as soon as possible.'

'SEA TRAGEDY ... Tension mounts.' A sodden placard on a news-vendor's stand slid past and Mark realized why Kirk was involved. The shipwreck had been mentioned twice on the radio and trouble was stirring in Northern Ireland. The tanker's look-outs stated that it seemed probable the two boats had rammed each other deliberately; they had sunk before the Greeks reached the scene; but the loss of life was unevenly balanced. Only the captain and one crew member of the *Loyal Apprentice* had died, while the bos'n was the sole survivor from the *Tyrconnell,* and Catholic fury was on the boil. But though he could understand why the incident should worry an Intelligence chief like Kirk, Mark could not for the life of him see any connection between a shipwreck and the Linsleat pollution, and certainly no reason why he should have been dragged back to London. How did nautical hooliganism and civil unrest concern a bacteriologist?

He cursed Kirk's summons, and thought of Tania again as he turned down the side road leading to Central Laboratories. Though he was glad she had decided to remain behind, he felt slightly apprehensive about her having accepted Meg's invitation to stay at the manor house till he returned.

'I don't want to be alone at the cottage, darling,' she had said. 'It may be neurotic of me, but I keep thinking of Ryder's body lying on the sofa ... thinking about the old judge, too. So silly, but I'd be much happier with Meg while you're away.'

'Don't worry about that, Mark.' She had smiled at his expression. 'What goes on between Meg and Willie Price is their business, and even if Bragshaw wasn't staying at the house, I'd be all right. Willie'd regret it if he laid a finger on me.'

'I'm sure he would, my sweet.' Mark's anxieties had lifted slightly. He had met Tania behind the Iron Curtain when she was secretary to Gregor Petrov, a departmental chief of the M.V.D., whose services to world disunity had earned him the title of Hero of the Soviet Union. Petrov was an amiable old gentleman nowadays, long retired, and it was through his good graces and influence that Tania had managed to leave Russia. But in his cups, Petrov sometimes boasted that he had caused more deaths than the cholera. Not a popular man, Gregor Petrov, and Tania had been employed as a body-guard as well as his secretary. She was well versed in unarmed combat and Mark felt confident that even Willie Price would be a poor match for her.

All the same, though he quite understood her reluctance to be on her own at the cottage, Tania could have got a room at the Rose and Leek, and he just didn't like the thought of her staying with Meg. No, he didn't like it one little bit, and his resentment against Kirk increased as he parked the car outside the laboratories.

'Ah, there you are at last, Sir Marcus.' His assistant, Paul Johnston, hurried across the entrance hall to greet him. 'Better late than never, as they say, and it's a pleasure to have you with us again.' He was a tall, gangling youth who had cultivated a lordly manner, and he took Mark's hat and coat with a flourish. A grave major-domo welcoming the master home. 'I hope you had a restful vacation, sir.'

'Don't try to be funny with me, Paul. I've hardly been away for five minutes.' Though Mark growled, he was very fond of Johnston, and there was some cause for amusement because this was the fifth time he had been called back from holiday in the last two years. 'Any idea what it's all about?'

'Only that there's quite a flap on and that trawler business has something to do with it. I tried to sit in, but our friend Professor Goater turfed me out. I gathered that he and the general are not on the best of terms. They're in Room 201 – and in some state of excitement, judging by the trays of black coffee they've been ordering.'

'Coffee. I could do with a cup myself, so you go and rustle it up, Paul.' Mark hurried past him. Already his ill humour was on the wane, because he loved the laboratory building with its stark, functional furnishings, the constant tang of chemicals and the faint hum of machinery on every corridor. Sometimes he thought of himself as a homing pigeon drawn back to the roost.

'Hullo at last, Mark.' Kirk got up from a chair as he entered the conference room, and Mark saw that there was indeed a flap on. The general's face was grey and tired, he could sense tension in the air, and though fans had kept the air free of smoke, the ashtrays were piled with cigar and cigarette butts. 'You took your time getting here.'

'I am not responsible for the traffic, Charles.' He nodded to the laboratory director, Professor Goater, a man whom he had consistently disliked since their first meeting several years ago. 'Nor have I any clear idea why you thought fit to interrupt my holiday, so may we get down to business?'

'We may indeed.' Kirk turned to a bearded man in naval uniform. 'This is Captain Cartwright and he has been giving us an eloquent dissertation on hydrodynamics.'

'Evening, Sir Marcus.' Cartwright was standing beside a chart hung from the wall. 'I hope I haven't appeared to be lecturing you, General Kirk, but I wanted to make it clear that there is a constant tidal flow which crosses the mouth of the Linsleat estuary – here.' He raised a crayon and drew a curving arrow across the map. 'This current continues for twelve and a half nautical miles before dispersing over Mulligan's Bank – here.' He circled the position.

'As you will have heard, Mulligan's Bank is the scene of the trawler collision, Sir Marcus, and I'd like to recap what I was saying, for your benefit.' Cartwright had a pleasant, breezy voice and Kirk was right in implying that he liked the sound of it. 'Though both the trawlers sank before the Greek tanker *Orchomenos* got close enough to lower her boats, the Greeks saved all the crew of the *Loyal Apprentice* except the master and an able seaman.

'But what about the *Tyrconnell*?' The captain paused for dra-

matic effect. 'Out of a crew of sixteen, only a single man and
a part of a man were picked up. The others were lost – either
sucked down by their ship or swept away by the current.'

'Thanks, Paul.' Johnston's arrival with the coffee had cut
the captain short and, despite Goater's obvious annoyance,
Mark motioned the young man to stay. 'Captain Cartwright,
I am sure that shipwrecks and currents are most interesting,
but they are hardly my province.'

'This one could be, Mark.' Kirk removed a cigar from
his mouth. 'You see, we are hoping that you may be able to
answer certain questions for us. Why was nobody seen on
the deck or bridge of the *Tyrconnell* before the collision took
place? Why did her skipper take no evasive action when he
saw the *Apprentice* pull across his bows? Why didn't her crew
put on lifebelts, lower rafts or make any attempt to save themselves? Why were there no survivors?'

'I thought there was one survivor, Charles.' Though Mark
was still bewildered, a little glimmer of light was starting to
glow. 'The bos'n.'

'Yes, the bos'n did survive for a time.' Kirk stared at the map
as if trying to picture the scene. 'His name was Brian Carlin
and he jumped over the side and was caught by the propeller.
He was unconscious when the Greeks picked him up, and he
was clutching a dismembered forearm in his right hand. He
died in hospital from head injuries three hours ago, and only
regained consciousness for a brief interval.'

'During which time he told a most ludicrous story that
the authorities very wisely suppressed, Sir Marcus.' Goater
looked angry. 'The man was delirious, General Kirk. He had a
compound skull-fracture, remember.'

'He also had an abdominal injury, received before the collision, that might have prolonged his life slightly.' Kirk turned
from the chart. 'I agree that the story sounds ludicrous and
the Ulster authorities were right to suppress it. Pity they didn't
act sooner. The gist of what Carlin said was leaked by a damn-

fool nurse before the ban came down, and appeared in the stop-press columns of two papers.'

'But whether he was delirious or not, his story tallies with the facts, gentlemen, and might account for the collision.'

'Quite so, Captain Cartwright, and that's why I asked Sir Marcus to cut short his holiday.' Kirk returned to his chair and pulled thoughtfully at his cigar for a moment. 'As I said, Carlin had injured his abdomen – he had fallen down a companion-way – and the master was heading back to Donegal at full speed. A bigoted fellow, apparently, who wouldn't trust one of his crew to a Northern Irish hospital.

'Anyway, Carlin had been confined to his berth and put on a liquid diet, and he was in his bunk when he heard the *Apprentice's* loud-hailer give warning. After his own ship did not respond to the warning he went out to investigate, and this is what he found, Mark.' Kirk's maimed hand tapped on the chair arm. 'The officers and men of the *Tyrconnell* were quite incapable of action and the vessel was out of control. Realizing that a collision was inevitable, Carlin picked up one of the ship's boys who was lying senseless on the deck and jumped overboard with him.'

'And the screw caught the poor devils? Carlin was weakened by his injury, probably in pain, and the propeller blades fractured his skull.' Mark felt awed by the seaman's endurance. He also felt excited because he fancied he knew why Kirk had sent for him. 'But Carlin held on to the boy even when he was unconscious.'

'All that was left of the boy; the right forearm, cut off at the elbow. Other bodies may be washed ashore, Mark, and Captain Cartwright will have divers sent down to the wrecks when the weather improves. But for the time being, that severed arm is the only evidence that might substantiate the rest of Carlin's story.'

'Story is the right word. A very tall story indeed.' Goater stood with his back to Kirk. 'It is a great pity that your holiday had to be interrupted, Sir Marcus, because I have already examined this so-called evidence and it conveys nothing. And I must remind you, General, that Carlin was delirious when he made his statement, and a seaman is not a doctor.' He sipped at a cup of black coffee, his forehead creased into a frown. 'I agree that it seems strange that the only survivor was a man who had been put on a liquid diet, but there must be some simple reason for the crew's behaviour. Maybe they were having a celebration and got tight. Saint Patrick's Day, perhaps?'

'Hardly that, Professor. The present month is September and the feast of Saint Patrick falls on March 17th.' Kirk looked at a calendar beside the door. 'And, though Carlin was not a medical man, one would expect a ship's petty officer to have had some first-aid training.'

'Will you please stop quibbling and get down to facts?' Mark's irritation had returned. 'Why is that boy's forearm so important?'

'That's what I want you to tell us, Mark.' Kirk spoke mildly but his eyes were troubled. 'According to Brian Carlin, the *Tyrconnell* was out of control because her crew were suffering from acute food poisoning.'

Chapter Nine

'Don't you hate that noise, Tania?' Megan was listening to a Skyrider throbbing through the low cloud that hung over the valley. 'Dan considered those exhaust frequencies were restful and inoffensive, but to me they're horrible – a chorus of banshees foretelling a death in the family.'

'I don't like the noise of a Skyrider, Meg, because it always reminds me of my . . . my accident.' For no reason she could think of, Tania hesitated over the word. The church clock had just struck eleven and the two women were walking in the garden before going to bed. 'But though the plane's sound is a bit eerie, surely it's not unpleasant, and your husband must have known what he was doing. Cedric told me that he did a lot of research to get the frequencies just right. Sent out questionnaires to test public reaction and so forth.'

'Does anybody really know what they're doing, my dear? Cedric and the other directors thought Dan's brain-child was a waste of time and money, but he got his way – as usual.' Meg looked at a lighted bedroom window. Bragshaw was still nursing his poisoned ankle, but he had sworn to return to work in the morning, whatever Travers might say. 'Dan always had his way. The board objected to Graebe's appointment at Linsleat, but he threatened to withdraw his capital if they vetoed it.

'Dan had two reasons for varying those exhaust frequencies, you know. He hoped to lessen annoyance, but he wanted advertisement as well. He once said that he regarded his engines as transmitters sending out call signs which would be heard all over the world and recognized as his.

'Yes, my late husband was a presumptuous man, Tania, and he usually got what he wanted. Maybe he got what he *deserved,* too.' Meg nodded towards the west. Cloud and darkness screened Allt y Cnicht, but Tania knew she was thinking of the mangled body that had lain below the crag. 'He proposed to me because he wanted to preserve the estate and, as people may have told you, I accepted him for the same reason.' She turned and they started to stroll back to the house.

'That's only partly true, though. I had to pay off my father's creditors, but I was very attracted to Dan when I first met him. He was on holiday, touring about the country at random, and had put up at the Rose and Leek for a night. Just one night was what he intended, but it stretched out into a month because he said that he'd fallen in love with the district. He used to go for long walks during the day, and every evening we'd meet for a drink or have dinner together and he'd tell me where he'd been. I've never known anybody so exuberant, so full of enthusiasm for a place. It was like being with a boy who'd just come home from a boarding school he hated.

'A boy who I thought was fond of me, but he grew up – he grew out of any nonsense like love even before we were married.' Meg stood aside to let Tania pass into the hall. 'Once the legal papers were signed and the estate was under his control, I realized that I was just a key which could be discarded because the door was open. Dan didn't care a rap for me – he didn't even want my body.'

'You mean that you were never lovers?' Tania was looking at an oil painting of Daniel Ryder above the fireplace. He sat at a table smiling cheerfully and he might have been announcing bumper trading results to a shareholders' meeting.

'Never once, my dear. Dan considered himself an honourable man and he attempted to do his marital duty, but I wouldn't let him touch me.' She spoke without any trace of bitterness. 'No, not because I realized why he had married me – not because I wasn't attracted to him. But when he came towards me on our wedding night, I looked into his eyes – and guess what I saw in them, Tania?' She lowered her own eyes to the floor. 'I didn't really expect love, but I thought he would want me physically. But there was no desire there, no passion at all. Just resignation and contempt. My husband regarded me as an inferior, a sort of sub-human creature. He would copulate with me out of duty but despise himself for it.'

'I'm sorry, Meg.' Tania laid a hand on her arm. 'He must have been insane – a megalomaniac.'

'I don't know what he was, my dear. I've been Dan's wife for nine years, but I've never known what made him tick.' Meg turned to draw the curtains. 'All I do know is that he was either completely insensitive or quite indifferent to other people's feelings.

'Think what he's done for the village. The hall, the hospital, the playground. He wanted respect and then offended everyone by providing a hostel for those hippies.'

'Meg, I have heard a rumour about the hippies.' Tania remembered what Willie Price had said before the snake whipped around Bragshaw's ankle. 'People are saying that your husband supplied them with drugs.'

'Are they indeed? What rubbish!' She closed the last curtain. 'Why should he have done that? Dan was a kindly philanthropist, remember. He saved my family home from the creditors, he built amenities for the people of Treflys, he gave the prodigal sons and daughters shelter.' Meg smiled cynically and then her manner became businesslike.

'He also allowed Rushton and his party to start their archaeological survey. But that is going to stop. I'm seeing the lawyers first thing in the morning and Rushton will get his marching orders. He'll be off my land before the day's out.'

'Meg, you're not serious? What harm are they doing? You don't really think that there is any truth in those legends?' Though Bragshaw had described Meg as 'a peasant under the veneer', Tania had not believed him till that moment. 'You surely don't pay any attention to the old wives' tales that Allt y Cnicht has some supernatural significance?'

'Don't I, my dear? I can assure you that I take them very seriously indeed. And so did Dan; that's why he invited Rushton to come here. He once told me that he almost knew the whole truth about Allt y Cnicht.' She nodded towards the library door. 'Said that the evidence was in there and I could examine it if I had the wits to open his safe. He was sneering as usual, but the safe's my property now and it'll be opened as soon as I get the combination from the makers.'

'Time's getting on, though, Tania. Would you like a nightcap?'

'No thanks, but I wouldn't mind something to read.'

'Help yourself.' Meg moved towards the staircase and then paused with her hand on the banisters. 'Tania, I would like to say how pleased I am that you decided to stay here. It was quite a gesture after what you witnessed the other night at

Willie's bungalow.' Meg's face seemed to grow smaller and she shivered with disgust. 'But I promise you that that was one single, repulsive incident which will never be repeated . . . never for as long as I live.' She turned and ran quickly up the stairs.

The Cambridge Ancient History . . . *The Directory of Directors* . . . *The Principles of Aerodynamics* . . . *The Avoidance and Cure of Diminishing Returns.* Tania studied the titles. Apart from the door and the window, and an old-fashioned combination safe standing between them, the library walls were completely shelved. But Ryder's reading matter looked pretty heavy-going.

An Approach to Economic Regeneration. She turned from the first section of shelves and looked at the safe. Ryder had challenged Meg to open it and the task did not seem too difficult. In Russia, Tania had once attended a course on lock construction and, with a stethoscope to help her, she fancied she could get the better of this one.

Why had Meg looked so stricken when she mentioned Willie Price, she wondered. Her disgust had appeared quite genuine, and she couldn't understand why. If Meg was really a masochist, surely she should have enjoyed the memory of Willie's huge brutal body heaving and pounding on top of her?

Ah, this looked more promising. She dismissed Megan's inclinations as she came to a shelf devoted to folklore. *The Arthurian Cycle* . . . *Legends of Northern Wales* . . . *A History of the Holy Grail* – and a little octavo volume bound in blue vellum and without a title on the cover. She pulled the book out and flicked it open. 'THE WATCHER OF THE HILLS. By His Honour Mr Justice Roberts. Published posthumously by Reaker and Jones, Swansea. Limited edition of 300 copies.'

The judge's thesis that they had discussed in the Leak. The book that he had never completed because somebody had crept into the cottage, overpowered him and tortured him to death. She sat down and turned to the Preface.

'The legend of Daran and his accursed and exiled followers has existed in the Treflys area from time immemorial: a sinister tale to frighten children and entertain visitors.' As Tania had expected, Roberts's style was pompous in the extreme. 'When I was a boy I had implicit belief in the Daran story, but when I became a man I put aside childish things – at least for a time.

'*In this age of reason and tolerance . . .*' The phrase was set in italics and she could imagine the scorn with which the old man had composed it. '*. . . In this century of liberal thought,* our ghosts and monsters have been banished. Grendel's dam is dead, the Plague Maiden no longer rides a corpse through the German forests, the Minotaur has gone to the slaughter house and will be served for Sunday lunch. To *educated* men and women, Daran was either a robber chief who once terrorized the district, or a product of the imagination.

'After I retired from the judiciary and returned to Treflys, I not unnaturally presumed that my neighbours would share these reasoned views, and certainly they claimed that this was the case. But I soon sensed that they were talented liars. Their belief in the Daran story was absolute, their fears boundless, and, being a man of inquiring disposition, whose trade was sifting truth from falsehood, I decided to examine the evidence for myself.

'Archaeological remains and recorded information are scant. Mentions of the legend occur in the Nantlyn Castle rolls and in a book of devotion compiled by the monks of Charwell Abbey, while the twelfth-century poet, Roger de Bors, composed a ballad entitled *Sire Daran and his elden, sicken folke.* Several troubadour verses also provide references and I shall detail all the sources in my glossary.

'Though this written information was, naturally, transcribed long after the events took place, it is interesting to note that much of it coincides with local tradition that has been handed down by word of mouth over the generations. This by itself cannot be regarded as reliable data, and it was by pure chance that I stumbled on evidence which led me to a verdict. This evidence will be reserved for the final chapters, but as I intend to play the role of prosecuting council, it seems fitting that I state my premise now.' Tania turned a page and stared at the next paragraphs, hardly able to believe her eyes. She had always suspected that Roberts must have been mentally abnormal, but he was a judge, a lawyer trained to weigh up evidence and arrive at the truth. It seemed incredible that such a man could have written the passage.

'There is not the slightest doubt that Allt y Cnicht, the Hill of the Knight, was once a place where great evil flourished. Nor is there any doubt that the fountain-head of that evil remains and is waiting to be released.'

Chapter 10

'Fair enough, Professor.' They had moved from the conference room to a laboratory and Mark stood before a bench, facing Goater and Captain Cartwright. 'The bos'n was a sick man when he heard the loud-hailer's warning and went out to investigate, and he was delirious when he made the allegation of food poisoning. But though we can't completely rely on his statement, witnesses from the *Loyal Apprentice* and the Greek tanker have testified that there was no sign of life aboard the *Tyrconnell*. Something must have affected the crew and poison is an obvious bet. What we have to do is to isolate the causative agent and find out where it came from.'

'I would have thought the source was obvious, Sir Marcus: Linsleat, of course.' Cartwright was pacing the laboratory as though it were a quarterdeck. 'There have been other outbreaks of illness originating from the estuary, and that current

I mentioned flows across its mouth towards Mulligan's Bank where the collision occurred. I've been shown the *Tyrconnell's* specifications and sea-water was used for everything except drinking. Polluted brine from Linsleat could easily have been pumped into her tanks and transmitted to the crew when they washed or shaved. But, because the bos'n was an odd man out, isn't it more likely that part of their catch was infected and they ate poisoned fish?'

'Which did not necessarily pick up the poison in or around the estuary itself.' Kirk was leaning heavily against a desk and he looked as if he could hardly keep his eyes open. 'D.R. Products have been transporting their waste materials out beyond the three-mile limit, remember.'

'Gentlemen,' Goater interposed, 'the D.R. plant was thoroughly inspected and their effluent has been analysed and proved harmless. The other establishments – the power station and so forth – are subject to inquiry, but as far as I'm concerned, there is no doubt that they will be exonerated.'

'There must be a culprit, however, so just whom have you in mind, Professor?' Mark remembered the scare stories written to the Irish newspapers. 'That the I.R.A. are responsible? That Russian trawlers are deliberately spreading pollution? Wouldn't that be carrying the cold war a bit too far?'

'There is no need to be flippant, Sir Marcus.' Goater nodded towards a folder on the table. 'You read my reports a few moments ago. Read them very cursorily in my opinion, but I trust you will respect the findings. I and my staff found nothing to show that the ship's boy had been poisoned – the effluent contained no toxic elements to account for any of the outbreaks.'

'Not in the samples you examined, Professor.' Mark suddenly felt he was back at Treflys hospital, trying to persuade George Travers to let him examine Ryder's body. Like Travers, Goater was professionally affronted. 'Who knows what effluent was discharged before the specimens were taken for analysis? And that suggests another possibility: a much more likely one.' He paused to ponder an idea that had just occurred to him.

'When the wildlife was first infected, the oysters were thought to have escaped, but later on they almost killed a number of people. Perhaps they were diseased all the time, but . . .' No, it was no good. He couldn't try to form his theory without evidence and he broke off with relief when Johnston beckoned him.

'You've got the slides ready, Paul? Right.' Mark bent over a microscope and twirled the fine adjustment. Part of a human being lay before him. A sliver of arterial tissue taken from a boy's forearm. Kirk had told him that the mangled arm had proved its owner a keen football fan: a circle of shamrocks and the slogan 'ROVERS – IRELAND'S GREATEST' were tattooed above the wrist. But could it tell them what had happened to the crew of the *Tyrconnell*?

'If it was food poisoning we can wash out ptomaine, salmonella and anything like that.' He squinted down at the slide. The cells had been stained purple to give them visibility, and they were rather beautiful. A tiny universe of suns and planets and distant stars floating in the dye. But they showed no trace of a virus infection – no suggestion that a bacillus had been present.

'In your report, you stated that he suffered from abnormally high blood pressure, Professor. A bit unusual for a sixteen-year-old boy, but I think you're right. Yes, there are definite signs of arterial thickening: extremely grave ones. Chances are that the poor little blighter wouldn't have lived long even if the propeller had missed him.' Johnston had prepared a fresh slide and he moved to another microscope.

'But what made those arteries fur up so quickly? The condition looks almost terminal and it must have been short-lived. Nobody with sclerosis like that could do manual work, and we can rule out any gradual build-up of cholesterol and fat deposits.' The picture was clearer on this slide and he could see how ill the boy had been. 'But acids produced by a sudden hormone disturbance might be responsible, if the hormone balance was upset violently enough. Not a release of noradrenalin, of course, but something of the kind.'

'Pure guesswork, Sir Marcus.' Goater breathed contempt down his neck. 'All we can possibly say is that the tissue shows symptoms of sclerosis.'

'Yes, I am guessing, Professor. But the fish and birds that became ill during the spring suffered from glandular and hormone disturbances. As did the oysters. Their systems contained an abnormally high percentage of iodine and that was what caused the Mansion House illness.

'If only we had some of the trawler's catch to examine.' He frowned at the absurdity of his wish, imagining the lifeboats heading past drowning men to pick up dead cod and mackerel.

'Thank you, Paul.' Mark returned to the first microscope. The slide told him no more than the others, but his theory was taking form and he considered the cycle of bubonic plague. *Bacillus pestis* living contentedly in the body of *Xenopsylla cheopis,* the rat flea, which suffers no ill effects from its presence. But the flea bites its host, and the rat is infected and crawls out of its hole to die. Then, about three days later, depending on climatic conditions, the flea, which relies on fresh blood for its existence, leaves the rat's carcass and attaches itself to man and other animals. After a further three days, the incubation period is complete and the breath and touch of an infected person can transmit the disease. An epidemic has begun.

Nothing resembling the plague bacillus was present here. But could something with a similar cycle have been at work, Mark asked himself. Something which was harmless when attached to lowly forms of life: algae, sea anemones, waterfleas. Something – he couldn't think of a better term – which became a scourge when transmitted to higher animals. Then, if these new hosts resisted the invasion by glandular and hormone modifications ... if they survived ... if the survivors had developed immunity, but still harboured the parasite ... they would be as dangerous as typhoid carriers – untroubled by their disease, but capable of passing it on with interest. If ...

A lot of 'ifs', and, as Goater had said, he was merely guessing. Mark straightened from the instrument and took out his cigarettes. All the same, the wild creatures that survived the Linsleat epidemic appeared to show glandular distortions, and hormone activity could have damaged the Irish boy's arteries.

'Thanks.' Johnston had lit his cigarette for him and he pulled deeply at it. The theory had possibilities, but a lot of work would be necessary before he could even discuss his suspicions. 'Professor Goater,' he said, 'I am sure the samples of D.R.'s effluent were most thoroughly analysed for inorganic poisons, but were they given a full ... a really full biological break-down?'

'They were not, and there was no reason why they should have been, Sir Marcus. Would you expect the waste products of a factory producing synthetic resins to contain living cells?'

'I don't know what I expect, but if there is some of that effluent still available, I'd like to have it sent up here, please.

'And there's something else I'd like, gentlemen: privacy.' He smiled apologetically. 'All I've got is a hunch and I just can't work before an audience.'

'Right, Paul, this is what we're going to need.' He watched Kirk lead the way to the door and started to dictate his requirements.

* * *

'Have a good feed, boys and girls, but fair's fair. Pay the bill by giving me a little information.' A line of fish tanks lay on the laboratory bench and Mark watched the commotion in the water. Infected water-fleas had been released and the minnows were snapping at them like blood-crazed barracuda.

The word 'infected' might be a boast, he thought bitterly. A quantity of the effluent had been introduced to algae just after midnight, the fleas had fed on the algae two hours later, now minnows were eating the fleas: the only way to test his theory that a living substance might be contained in the effluent – an organism which did not trouble primitive life forms but became a scourge as it passed up the social scale. But it was eight o'clock in the morning and his hopes were on the wane. This was the sixth batch of fish which had been treated, and so far there had been no reaction at all.

'Still negative, Paul?' He crossed over to Johnston who was stationed before an electron microscope. They had each allowed themselves an hour's rest since the experiments began, but he felt tired and dull-witted.

'I just don't know, sir. For a moment I thought I'd spotted something a bit unusual on the top right-hand corner, but I can't be sure.'

'Let's have a look.' Mark bent over the eyepiece and studied a sliver of tissue taken from a goldfish that had been fed six hours ago. As far as he could see, the creature appeared to have been quite healthy, and in the tank it had come from, its neighbours were drifting contentedly through the water.

'Just a moment, though.' He stared at the place Paul had indicated. Was there a slight distortion of the cells there? Did that tiny blur on the slide indicate the presence of organic illness? Possibly so, but probably not, and in any case the image was too small and indistinct to speculate on.

He walked over to the window and raised the blind. Something had ravaged the wildlife at Linsleat, something had caused the oysters to store toxic quantities of iodine, something must have been responsible for the trawlermen's illness. When Kirk and the others had left the laboratory, Mark had felt fairly confident that a micro-organism had been the culprit; but now, with the morning sun climbing over London, his confidence had evaporated. He didn't know what they were up against and he almost wished that he had ignored Kirk's summons and remained in Wales.

' "Sire Daran and his elden, sicken folke".' He had rung Tania while he took his break, she had told him about the judge's book of folklore, and quite out of the blue the quotation occurred to him and restored his hopes. Sickness was not a myth to be regarded with superstitious dread, but a physical condition that could always be tamed by isolation of the parasite responsible. At some point of time the enemy must come into the open and be recognized.

But time was running out. If there was a virus or a bacillus at work, it obviously acted quickly and should have revealed its presence long ago. Just an hour and a half before the trawlers collided, the *Tyrconnell* had radioed her owners, and, apart from the bos'n's injury, she had reported that nothing was amiss.

'Come on, damn you. Just give me a clue that I'm on the right track.' He crossed to a tea trolley, scowling at the tanks as he passed them, as though their occupants were deliberately frustrating him. Not only goldfish and minnows had been treated; twelve tanks were ranged along the bench and they housed eels and crabs, lobsters and terrapins. Each species had been fed on algae or water-fleas and they all appeared to be in the best of health.

'Let's take a break, Paul.' Mark poured out the tea and frowned at his watch. After another couple of hours he would have to admit defeat.

'May I make a suggestion, Sir Marcus?' Johnston took a cup from him. 'We seem to be getting nowhere, so why not try a long shot? A direct injection of the effluent into a mammal.'

'Paul, Paul, why persecutest thou me?' The joke was automatic, but he was too tired to feel any humour. 'Haven't you taken in anything I've told you? A mammal would suffer no ill effects at all. I saw Daniel Ryder drink the stuff, and though he died later, it wasn't the effluent that killed him.' The sounds of the room droned through Mark's head while he spoke: pumps supplying oxygen to the tanks, fans humming in the ceiling, the murmur of traffic from the window. There was also a fourth noise which he couldn't recognize.

'If there is a biological element contained in the effluent, it must be in a very primitive state and needs time to develop itself. An organism which evolves and increases in virulence while passing from one host to another. A process of accumulated incubations, you might say.

'And judging by our results so far, you might also say that I'm talking through my hat. For all I really know, an act of God may be responsible. Or perhaps a computer has run amok and programmed the power station reactor to contaminate the estuary water? Maybe those letter-writers hit on the truth and we're up against a synthetic virus released by the I.R.A. or Russian spy trawlers. Or what about Arab dhows? Being a Jew, I might swallow that one.' He grinned mirthlessly again.

'What's your guess, Paul?

'No . . . no. Keep quiet for a moment.' He raised his hand as Johnston started to answer. What was that sound that he couldn't place? Where was it coming from? A noise that made him think of a carpet being beaten in a next-door garden. Had one of the pumps gone wrong? Had a fan-blade worked loose?

'Paul, look. Just look, boy.' Mark's eyes had been darting around the room, but now they were fixed on the bench and widening with triumph. The minnows still hunted their prey, the eels twirled lazily through the water, the crustaceans and terrapins were enjoying their quiet pleasures. But in the tank nearest to him, the tank into which the fleas had been first introduced, he saw the proof that his hunch had paid off. The sound was caused by seven goldfish that were flapping crazily against the glass, while their three neighbours floated lifelessly on the surface.

Chapter Eleven

'An objectionable fellow, that, Tania.' Dr Travers watched Bragshaw's car proceeding down the drive. 'Though he may have a heart like an ox, adder bites are unpleasant things and when I advised the fool to rest up a bit longer he more or less told me to go to hell.'

'Self-important brute. Now that Dan Ryder's out of the way, he fancies he's the great tycoon. Imagines the firm will go to pot without his mighty brain to guide it.'

'Well, if he wants to go to work with a poisoned leg, that's his lookout and I hope it gives him hell.' The car was out of sight and Travers walked back into the hall. 'Any idea when Meg will be home, my dear?'

'Early afternoon, she said. Willie Price drove her to the solicitors' in Bangor.'

'And when she gets back the fur will begin to fly. I'd like to see Rushton's face when he gets his marching orders.' The doctor chuckled maliciously. 'Those young layabouts in the barn, too. The valley will be a cleaner place without them. Why Dan allowed them to stay there beats me.'

'Do you think they are on drugs, George?' Once again Tania recalled Willie's accusation against Ryder. 'The hard stuff?'

'I shouldn't think so. It's common knowledge that they smoke hash and take pep pills, but I'd have known about it if any of them were on mainliners. Heroin soon shows its results.' Travers walked through into the sitting-room, where he had been examining Bragshaw. 'Something very rum about the hippies when you think about it. Must be about nine months since they came here, but I've never seen one of them at my surgery. Yes, very strange. They look physical wrecks but they don't get ill. Maybe squalor and idleness are aids to health.

'And talking about health aids reminds me that an offer of refreshment is due.' He nodded at the cocktail cabinet. 'As Meg's out it's your job to play hostess.'

'Of course. Brandy as usual, George?'

'No, a bit early for that; but a spot of sherry should wash the taste of Bragshaw out of my mouth.' Travers followed her across to the cabinet. It was his half-day, and he had arrived on a motorcycle and wore a shabby tweed jacket similar to the one Ryder had worn on the day he died. But a faint odour of antiseptic hung about him and made Tania think of Mark far away at Central Laboratories. Mark had sounded depressed when they spoke on the phone and had not talked about his work, which usually meant that things were going badly. 'No, darling,' he had said, 'I can't explain now, and I don't want to. I just want to relax for a bit, so tell me about yourself. Everything all right – no trouble with Meg or Willie?

'Judge Roberts's book? That should be pleasant bedtime reading, but is there any logic in it?' Mark had fallen silent when she described what she had read, and she imagined they had been cut off till he answered her again. 'Yes, I'm still here, darling, but I was thinking of that title you mentioned. "Sire Daran and his elden, sicken folke." I rather like that.'

'Thank you.' She had poured out the sherry, and Travers drank greedily and smacked his lips. 'Excellent. One thing in Ryder's favour was that he kept a decent cellar.

'Ah, you've been having a look at that, have you?' Tania had left the book lying on a table and he crossed over to it. 'What do you make of Roberts's incomplete masterpiece?'

'That he must have been going out of his mind.' Tania had felt restless without Mark and she had sat up reading into the small hours. But she still hadn't finished the treatise. Certain passages had been so muddled that she had had to keep reading back through the text, and after breakfast she'd taken a map from the library to check the topographical details. 'From about the middle of the book the style and material get more and more disjointed at every page.'

'He was pretty disjointed himself when he got to the middle, Tania, but were his premises correct? That's what interests me.' Travers picked up the volume. 'That chap Rushton and his crew seem convinced that the area was once inhabited by a noble and talented race who degenerated over the centuries and were cruelly massacred by their neighbours.

'But our locals are terrified of the legend and Roberts, a highly intelligent man, shared their feelings.' He flicked through the pages, reading the odd passage aloud. ' "Does the influence of these people remain? A tainted species who ruled by fear – worshippers of a satanic man-god – spreaders of sickness existing in harmony with rats, vipers and poisonous insects, creatures always associated with disease." ' The doctor grinned and helped himself to one of Megan's cigarettes. 'Maybe it was a descendant of their pet adders that got its fangs into Bragshaw.'

'If there is any grain of truth in the story, George, the judge may have been right in saying that the Celts were terrified of them.' Tania recalled one of Roberts's footnotes: 'The usual Celtic practice was to incorporate children and female captives into their society, but they attempted to wipe out every member of Daran's tribe.'

'And failed miserably it seems. This is how one medieval chronicler ends the story.' Travers read aloud again. ' "In the early hours did they surprise the old ones and bind them strongly with cords. In the late noonday they did lead them up to the mountain which had once housed their strongholds and temples." Yes, the style does sound a bit pretentious. This must have been written in dog Latin and Roberts tried to reproduce the feeling in modern English and made a hash of it.' The doctor pulled at his cigarette and continued. ' "When that place was reached, they did lay the being named Daran on a slab and did stone him with his creatures looking on. But the fiend could not be killed by their art. Even with the body broken in the six places that prophecy required, did Daran cry out to his fellows in their ancient language. First chiding them for their weakness and then foretelling that they must wander in isolation; friendless and lost till strength and wisdom were reborn in them and the day of vengeance had come to pass." That's all there is of that, but a poet called de Bors finishes the yarn.' Travers laid down the book and looked at the map spread out on the table. 'According to de Bors, the prisoners were suddenly turned into ravens and flew off across the hills, while the Celts rather weakly gave up trying to kill Daran and buried him alive.

'What about giving me one for the road, my dear.' He gulped back the remains of the sherry. 'I'm going to do a spot of fishing this afternoon and will miss my usual session at the pub.'

'Of course.' Tania refilled his glass. 'There's also another version of the story which says that the bodies of Daran's people did die, but their spirits left them and possessed a number of the Celts who became insane and were banished from the tribe.'

'Yes, a sort of Gadarene swine affair.' Travers ran his finger along the map as if tracing a route. 'An awful lot of tosh from beginning to end. Or so I once thought.'

'You mean you don't think it's tosh now?' Tania laid the glass beside him, remembering his words in the pub. 'You honestly think there's some truth in the story? You believe Roberts had reason to think that Allt y Cnicht has some supernatural association?'

'All I know is that there's never smoke without fire, my dear.' His index finger was rigid at a point on the map. 'I also know it was that mountain which drove Judge Roberts round the bend.

'Oh, he'd always been a bit strange, obsessed with sin and punishment, but he had a good logical brain till a few months before he was murdered.' The doctor raised his glass, but he only took a sip this time. 'I went to have supper with Roberts one evening and I've rarely seen a man so changed. His speech was rambling and incoherent at times; though it was a coldish night he was sweating, and he kept getting up from the table and pacing around the room. When we were having coffee his hand shook so badly that he dropped the cup, and then without warning he burst into tears. Just imagine that, Tania. A High Court judge, notorious for severity, weeping like a frightened child.' As if reliving the incident, Travers paced the room as Roberts had done.

'To cut the story short, the old boy finally pulled himself together and told me that he'd had a shock. He'd been walking along the crags above the dynamite store and located a fissure; not a cave, just a narrow crack that he could barely squeeze through. There were some curious marks – carvings I think he said – on the rocks, which he photographed with a flash-bulb, and the end of the passage was blocked by a man-made wall which he started to dislodge – only started to dislodge. Before he'd loosened a single stone, he turned and ran like a bat out of hell.

'No, he wouldn't say what frightened him. Something he saw or stumbled against, perhaps – something he sensed. That was all I could get out of him, though he pulled out a map and showed me where the place was. He also produced a Bible and made me swear not to reveal the location to anybody till he'd worked out what the marks on the rocks signified. He said that once his book was finished, people would know exactly what had existed on that mountain.

'Sorry, my dear, but that's a promise I intend to keep.' He shook his head when Tania prompted him. 'As I told you, I don't know what the judge experienced at that man-made wall, and I'm not going to give anybody else the chance to share it.' Travers returned to the table and finished his drink.

'From that day the old chap's imagination got the better of his reason and his mind ran down. The story of Daran ceased to be a myth and he honestly believed that some evil force was located on Allt y Cnicht. He also considered himself a crusader whose mission was to expose that force and destroy it. To give himself the energy to write, he almost lived on purple hearts, and he took sleeping-pills because he was too nervous to go to bed without them.

'No, he didn't get them from me, my dear.' Travers smiled wryly and picked up his medical bag. 'Mr Justice Roberts, a man who regarded criminals as personal enemies, made regular trips to Liverpool and bought his comforts under the counter.

'He may have experienced nothing in that fissure, of course. I'm no psychiatrist, but perhaps he had always suffered from some mental illness that had lain dormant since infancy. An aberration that just happened to be triggered off by the atmosphere of the place; claustrophobia, perhaps. But whatever the truth, it ruined him, and the drugs would have killed him if his murderer hadn't got to him first. It also gave yours truly one hell of a shock to see a High Court judge in tears, and I think that that part of the mountain may be a good place to keep away from.'

'And *I* think I know where the place is, George.' Tania pointed at the map. 'For the last few minutes you've been either staring at this spot here or looking through the window along the north face of Allt y Cnicht.'

'Then take my advice and put it out of your mind, my dear.' Travers spoke gruffly and then smiled. 'I'll get along and see if the fish are rising now, and you forget everything I've said. Thanks for Meg's sherry and my regards to Mark when he gets back. Tell him that he was a young whippersnapper to query my post mortem on Ryder, but no hard feelings.' He smiled again and moved off.

A good place to keep away from. Meg had used a similar phrase last night, Tania remembered. Why should otherwise rational people hold such irrational views about Allt y Cnicht, she wondered. Emrys Hughes, Judge Roberts, the Ryders, Rushton and his archaeologists; now the usually cynical George Travers.

Though George seemed to be becoming a bit senile: first quarrelling with Mark and then forgetting the tools of his profession. Tania picked up the stethoscope he had left lying on a chair and hurried after him. But before she was halfway across the hall she stopped and glanced at the library door, with the instrument dangling in her hand.

Daniel Ryder had told Meg that if she opened his safe, she would know what had really happened on Allt y Cnicht, and with a stethoscope that combination should not be too difficult to work out. Tania waited till she heard the doctor's motorcycle drive away and then walked into the library.

*　*　*

The safe looked formidable; the whole alphabet was included on its dial, but only a fraction of the letters would be connected with the locking mechanism. Five or six probably, and an alphabetical sequence was usually easier to break than a combination of numbers. Tania knelt before the door and fitted the stethoscope into her ears. Few people can remember a disjointed string of letters and there was a good chance that a word or a proper name might contain the secret. She placed the stethoscope pad beneath the dial and got to work.

A! That was a stroke of luck. At the first turn there had been a positive click and she entered the letter in her diary. *B*. Another click, but one that denoted failure and the *A* tumbler had returned to the locked position. She released it again and began to go patiently through the alphabet.

. . . *X – Y – Z*. She had been over-confident and this lock could prove a devil. Tania looked at her watch. Twenty minutes had passed, and all she had so far were the two letters *A* and *V*. Idle curiosity had prompted her safe-breaking attempt and she was starting to regret it. Megan Ryder intended to have the safe opened for herself, but if she returned to find that a guest had forestalled her she might not appreciate it. Tania removed the stethoscope from one ear and listened for the sound of a car coming up the drive.

A – V – A. Another positive reaction at last and a girl's name was entered in the diary. She pulled at the door handle with small hopes that it would respond and then stood up and lifted a pocket dictionary from the shelves. If the combination was an actual word, there might be a short cut.

'Avant – avarice – avast – avaunt.' Each sequence spelt failure and the little dictionary was useless. She laid it aside and worked through the alphabet again.

'*A – V – A – T*.' The *T* had registered a hit, but she couldn't think of any word starting that way. Perhaps a proper name or a foreign word, and the encyclopaedia might help.

Yes, this could be it. Her eyes lit up at the reference. '*AVATAR* (Sanskrit *avatara,* descent) signifies in Hindu mythology the descent of a deity . . .' She replaced the volume, hurried back to the safe and dialled. One by one the tumblers were released and the job was done. She pulled lightly at the handle – and Daniel Ryder's secrets lay open for her inspection.

At first glance there appeared to be nothing revealing about the contents of the safe; certainly nothing connected with the Daran legends. Apart from a portable tape-recorder, the shelves were stacked with cardboard folders, neatly labelled to show that they were concerned with business matters. She glanced at her watch again and sorted almost idly through them.

Architectural plans for the chemical plant at Linsleat . . . A prepared balance-sheet for Rydercraft Aviation and its subsidiary companies . . . Further experiments to eliminate sound-disturbance on the Model II Skyrider: five thick folders filled with graphs and drawings and technical data that meant nothing to her were devoted to that subject. She was about to replace them when a document written in Russian attracted her attention.

Hadn't Cedric Bragshaw mentioned this? The specifications of a Soviet-built airspeed indicator that was to be fitted to the new planes and which he and the other directors considered a needless expense.

'My very dear friend and comrade.' There was a note pencilled across the foot of the page and Tania frowned. Surely that was rather a strange way for a Russian civil servant to address a British businessman? 'On Plate 5 (enclosed) you will see that the instrument has been modified, and I am confident that the added detail will operate to our mutual satisfaction.' The signature belonged to somebody called V. I. Demchinsky.

'Our mutual satisfaction'. Another curious wording, and hadn't she heard the name V. I. Demchinsky not so long ago? Tania frowned again and then nodded. Gregor Petrov had once mentioned it in a letter to her: 'The British Secret Service can hardly congratulate themselves on the disgraceful Demchinsky affair.'

And hadn't Charles Kirk brought up the matter when he dined with them some weeks back? Yes, he'd been furious because one of the Sunday newspapers had published a lurid version of the story and implied that his department was incompetent.

Vladimir Ivanovich Demchinsky. The details were coming back to her. Demchinsky was a senior designer at an aircraft components factory near Leningrad and he had been sent to East Germany on a lecture tour. According to the newspaper, he had contacted a British agent and stated a wish to defect to the West. Because he was a key scientist with information to sell, help had been offered and the arrangements made. But somebody blundered, the V.O.P.O. came on the scene and

Demchinsky had been riddled with bullets as he mounted the Berlin Wall. Technically the escape succeeded. He reached his goal but died an hour later in a West Berlin hospital.

'My very dear friend and comrade ... added detail ... our mutual satisfaction ...' Was the note a code informing Daniel Ryder of what Demchinsky intended? Had Ryder negotiated for the airspeed indicators in the hope that he could make personal contact with Demchinsky and persuade him to defect? The man would have been a valuable asset to Rydercraft Aviation.

What was this? Tania opened a child's exercise-book that lay beneath the Russian document. Its pages were covered with signs and symbols that might be technical data, and they conveyed nothing to her. But here and there disjointed passages of handwriting had been included.

'Concentration difficult today ... memory faulty ... must record current progress as best I can, however ...' Tania turned her head towards the window. There was the car returning and Meg might not be pleased with her activities. She'd better shut the safe and wait for a suitable moment to tell her that she'd solved the combination.

'Our young protégés continue to thrive and suspect nothing.' She had been about to replace the book when she noticed the passage. Did it refer to the young people Ryder had housed in the farm building, perhaps? If so, what was it that they might suspect?

'To date, thirty-nine of our very dear friends and comrades have been reunited, and with our Creator's help we are certain that one day the Master will be revealed and the operation commence.' The car had drawn up, but Tania still bent over the page. *Very dear friends and comrades.* The same way that Demchinsky had addressed Ryder.

More signs ... more meaningless symbols, and then: 'Up to the present the call has been answered as follows. October 3rd, 1967, Charles Conrad ... December 12th, 1967, Jane Wallace

. . . May 19th, 1968, Vladimir Demchinsky . . .' Feet had crossed
the gravel, the doorbell was ringing and Tania replaced the
book with the tail-end of the list burning behind her eyes.
Apart from Demchinsky's, the early names meant nothing to
her and she had hardly registered them in her memory. But
she would never forget the date of the last entry. It was the day
on which she had lost her baby and the name that followed
was Michael Turner.

★　　★　　★

'Good morning, Lady Levin.' She had opened the door to find
Professor Rushton waiting in the porch. He was dressed in
his working uniform of overalls and thick boots, and looked
as much the cinema frontiersman as ever. 'Is Mrs Ryder at
home?'

'Meg's out, I'm afraid, but I don't suppose she'll be long.'
Tania shook her head absent-mindedly. She still felt numbed
by the sight of Turner's name. What did the list mean? What
was the call that had been answered? 'Would you like to wait
for her, Professor?'

'Thank you. I can't stay long, but it is essential that Mrs
Ryder and I come to an understanding.' He walked past her
without remembering to wipe his boots, and they left a trail
of dust on the carpet. His face and hands were also grimy and
there was a bandage around his right wrist. He appeared tense
and angry and also slightly pathetic. The homestead was in
real danger, and for once old granddaddy seemed at a loss to
outwit the cattle barons.

'I don't know if you are aware of what is taking place, Lady
Levin. But in case I have to leave before Mrs Ryder returns, I
would ask you to give her this and deliver a verbal message.'
He reached in his overalls and produced an envelope. 'Tell her
that we'll fight her blasted peasants to the last ditch.

'But you have no idea what I'm talking about, have you?'

He registered Tania's bewilderment with his striking blue eyes – eyes that were inflamed with slate dust or emotion. 'But you do know the local people's attitude towards our work. Since they realized we were serious students, they have been uncooperative, hostile, and openly insolent at times. That is their privilege. But now physical violence has been threatened and I have no doubt that Mrs Ryder must have ordered it.

'An hour ago, Emrys Hughes and about a dozen other louts turned up at the site and told us to stop work. They informed us that Mrs Ryder wanted us off her land and we had till tomorrow morning to pack up and leave the district. If we refused, they promised to steal dynamite from the explosives store and destroy our camp. Some of them had shotguns and dogs, and when I naturally told Hughes to go to hell his brute flew at me.' He held up his wrist and Tania saw that blood was seeping through the bandage.

'I'm sorry, Professor.' She did feel very sorry indeed, because Rushton was obviously a visionary whose search for the pre-Celtic culture had become an obsessive dream: a compulsion as strong as love or alcoholism. 'But, though I'm sure Meg didn't persuade Hughes and the others to threaten you, she does want you off her land and she'll be within her legal rights. She told me that according to their marriage settlement, the estate became hers after her husband's death.'

'True enough, but there's something she hasn't told you and may not know herself.' He opened the envelope and held out a Photostated document. 'Two clauses were added to that marriage settlement. The land does belong to Mrs Ryder, but no persons may be evicted if they are engaged in serious historical research or subsisting on charity. That obviously includes our party and those unfortunate children Dan gave shelter to.'

'I see.' Though veiled by legal jargon, the document showed that he had stated the facts correctly. 'Ryder had these clauses inserted before he and Meg were married ... before he heard that you wanted to start your research ... before he decided to convert the farm building into a hostel. What a strange thing to have done.' Tania was still considering the papers she had seen in the safe. 'How well did you know Daniel Ryder, Professor?'

'Not well socially. His wife frowned on our relationship. I believe she disliked me from the word go, and this is only the third or fourth time I have set foot in the house. But Dan and I could have become very close, I think.' Rushton's tone was guarded as if he disliked a show of emotion. 'He had such an inquiring mind ... such a thirst for knowledge, and I imagine we might have grown to be very good friends.

'But what's the good of talking about what might have been? Dan is dead; he can't help us any more, and though that woman has no legal power to turn us away, she can make things very difficult.' He gave a despairing gesture and smoothed back his unruly white hair.

'Using dynamite was a childish threat, of course, but those peasants regard her as something akin to a feudal overlord. If she wants a vendetta, they'll provide one and I can imagine how it'll be carried out. Rocks will fall, fires start, men and women will get beaten up in the dark. Yes, those are the sneak-thief methods Mrs Ryder will have in store for us.'

'Why not ask her to stop them, Professor?' Rushton's anger had been replaced by sadness and Tania felt more and more sympathetic towards him. 'Meg is terrified of the Daran legend and you can't blame her. Like all the local people she's had it rammed down her throat since the cradle. She honestly believes that there is a supernatural force surrounding Allt y Cnicht which your research might unleash. But she's also an educated woman, and if you reasoned with her ... if you could persuade her how groundless her fears are ...'

'You are very kind, Lady Levin, but Mrs Ryder is past reason, I'm afraid.' He moved across to the window. 'That story has not merely troubled her since childhood, she's been haunted by it for centuries. Her ancestors were the people who attempted to destroy and obliterate the old civilization, and fear is lodged in their blood like a hereditary disease, like haemophilia.

'No, we must just stand on our rights and resist the persecution, and that is what I came here to tell Mrs Ryder. We have only a short time left, our progress has been slow, but before this week's out we must ... we are determined to reach our goal and it will take more than her yokels to stop us.'

'The end of the week – you have only a few more days.' Tania had been about to ask him what the urgency was, and then remembered that most of his team were on vacation and would have jobs waiting for them. 'Professor, you say that your progress is slow, and I wonder if you've been concentrating on the wrong area. Apparently Judge Roberts based his conclusions on something he found much higher up the mountain.'

'What?' Rushton swung round. His wrinkled face showed no anger and no despair now. He looked like a child pleading for assurance that Santa Claus does exist. 'You mean that after Georges Destin asked you to search the cottage you found written evidence: papers – notes that the judge had hidden?'

'Nothing like that. But about a month before he died Mr Roberts showed Dr Travers a map and told him that somewhere above the dynamite store he'd located a cave ... a fissure with carvings on the rock, and a man-made wall at the end of it.'

'Carvings – perhaps runic inscriptions. We know that he did photograph an inscription of some kind, but if there were others, the whole puzzle might fit together. And he found a wall – a man-made wall.' Rushton looked out through the window again. The lower slopes of Allt y Cnicht were clear, though mist still clung around the summit. 'There is a tradition that after Daran was stoned the Gaels took him to some holy place – one of his own temples, perhaps. But there could be many such locations and we have been virtually working at random. But now . . . now, at last . . .' He swung round and Tania was touched by his eagerness. The promise had been given and Santa was due down the chimney on Christmas Eve. 'Thank you, Lady Levin. God bless you, because this is just the kind of lead I have been praying for. Do you think Travers remembers the exact spot the judge pointed out to him?'

'I'm sure he does, but he may not tell you. He made a promise to keep the information a secret.'

'Then you will have to use your persuasive powers, Professor Rushton.' Megan Ryder stood framed in the kitchen doorway. The car must have returned by the back drive, and, though they had not heard her arrival, she had obviously been standing there for some time and had heard a good deal of their conversation. 'George Travers is a greedy old man and the almighty dollar might loosen his tongue.' She smiled broadly as if some private joke had occurred to her.

'I have seen my lawyers, Professor, and they have made Daniel's dispositions quite clear to me. I have also heard that Emrys Hughes and his friends threatened you and you have my assurance that nothing of the kind will happen again.

'You're a lucky man, aren't you? As Tania has said, all you need is a chat with George Travers and you're home and dry. The truth about this noble civilization – this master race my people destroyed – will be revealed in all its glory.

'But though you may have luck and Daniel's blessing, I am not forced to entertain you, Professor Rushton.' Meg's smile vanished and she pointed to the door. 'So, get the hell out of my house.'

Chapter Twelve

'Hark, I hear the foe advancing . . . Barbary steeds are proudly prancing.' Wire cages had joined the fish tanks in the laboratory, and Mark was watching a battle. 'Spearheads in the sunlight glancing . . .' He hummed the words while he stooped sideways to get a better view of the slaughter. '. . . Glitter through the trees.'

The foe were advancing all right and in a very complex and wonderful manner; he had seen the invaders quite clearly on the last slide Paul Johnston had prepared. They were dead, of course. The stain added to the specimen to produce visibility had killed them, and their lifeless hordes floated in a drop of liquid no bigger than a pin-head. But Mark knew that, when alive, they had been as terrible as any human army with its tanks and guns and aircraft.

'From the rocks rebounding . . . Hear their war cry sounding . . .' Six of the rats had died, three were slowing down, but one appeared to have come to terms with its illness: the big piebald animal nearest to him was cleaning its fur beside the fleshless skeleton of a goldfish – one of the baits by which poison had been delivered.

'Less than three hours since the poor brutes were fed, Paul. The process accelerates with each host. It was over six hours before we noticed any change in the fish.' He turned to Kirk who had come back after hearing of their progress.

'You asked me whether we're dealing with a virus or a bacillus, Charles, and I couldn't tell you. Now I suspect that the joker is some minute form of amoeba, but I'm only guessing.' Mark grimaced at the tanks and the cages. He had to destroy one form of life to gain the knowledge to save another, or try to save it; but animal experiments always sickened him. Some of the goldfish had recovered and were swimming normally, but another rat was dying and lay panting against the wire. 'But whatever genus the parasite belongs to, I'm not guessing about its life-cycles.' He gave the ghost of a smile. 'We have a social climber to deal with.

'When the Linsleat outbreak was first noticed, D.R. Products were trying to perfect a new fibre based on synthetic resins, and I think that's what caused the trouble. During the experiments they must have accidentally stumbled on a colloid containing protoplasm, the source of all living tissue. This would have appeared sterile and gone undetected in the laboratory, but when released into the estuary, cell production began.

'Because Daniel Ryder suffered no ill effects when he drank the effluent, it is clear that the protoplasm is harmless to man; probably our antibodies destroy it. But in the lower creatures the substance flourishes. A micro-organism is born and he starts to creep up the social ladder.' Mark nodded towards the nearest tank.

'*Cladecera,* water-fleas, were the first hosts I provided, and though some of them died, the majority recovered and became immune but capable of transmitting their parasites to other species.

'Fish came next, the process is repeated, and our friend becomes stronger and more virulent though still too small to be observed under a microscope. But when the third incubation has been achieved, one can see him all right and he's a real monster.' Mark pointed towards the piebald rat which had finished its cleaning operations and was chasing its tail like a kitten. 'That chap's survived all right. Like a diphtheria or typhoid carrier, he's developed personal immunity and will suffer no inconvenience. But if his complaint was passed on to a still higher animal, such as man, I don't think there'd be many survivors. The parasite has reached maturity in that rat's system, and with a few drops of his blood Paul and I could grow cultures to wipe out half the population of London.'

'A series of physical reincarnations, each stronger than its predecessor. That's pretty gruesome, Mark.' Kirk drew back from the cage as if fearing that the wire might suddenly part and the rat fly at him. 'But just a moment, old boy. Surely you're wrong about there being no survivors? Those people who ate the oysters all recovered.'

'That was quite different. Obviously the oysters housed the parasite and became resistant, but it's definite that the human illness was caused by their high iodine content. The organism must have been in the second stage of development and powerless against our antibodies.

'What the hell am I saying?' Mark looked savagely at a line of plastic saucers on the table. Each saucer contained a culture of the things he had seen under the microscope, and every culture was thriving and reproducing itself faster than he had imagined possible. ' "Obviously ... it's definite ... must have been." Nothing's obvious, Charles, nothing's definite, and how conceited can I get? We know that the little devil evolves by serial incubations, and becomes more inimical stage by stage. We know that it kills by increasing its victims' glandular and hormone activity. But that's all we damn well do know, and there's something almost uncanny about the cycle. The reproductions are so regular, so well-organized. Almost as if there was an intelligence behind them.'

'Which there very well may be, Mark, and I'm surprised you haven't considered the possibility before.' Kirk laid his briefcase on the desk. 'For a Yid you're a pretty trusting sort of blighter, but I've got a nasty suspicious mind. When you reported your progress to me, my suspicions were increased and now you've confirmed them.' He pulled a folder from his case and nodded at the saucers. 'Yes, Mark, there is an intelligence behind those creatures, and it's aim is murder: mass murder by a man-made mutant.' He moved to the door. 'I now intend to persuade the powers-that-be to act on my suspicions, and while I'm telephoning you might care to read that dossier.'

'It's our turn to take the offensive at last.' Mark turned to Johnston. His suspicions were too engrossing for him to concentrate on Kirk's for the moment, and his eyes switched from the cages to the saucers and back again. Only the piebald rat was still alive, but the slaughter had been justified and the dead animals had told him a great deal. He had a vague picture of the foe that was advancing, he could start to hit back and his spirits rose at the prospect. In a few minutes the cultures would be attacked by his own armies and they must put paid to the little monsters from Linsleat. 'You know the type of antibiotics we'll need, Paul, so have the full range sent up.

'Now, what's this about?' He opened Kirk's file and a photograph stared up at him from above a line of thick print, HANS GRAEBE ... So, that was it. A dossier prepared by the Immigration Department when the German applied for a British work permit.

'Born Dresden 1914 ... Father a dentist, mother an elementary schoolmistress ... Hitler Youth 1930 ... Dresden University 1932, Berlin University 1936 ... Membership of Nazi Party 1937 ... Excused military service on the grounds of priority ... Degrees obtained ...' Mark raised his eyebrows, because Graebe's academic qualifications were certainly impressive. He could quite see why he had escaped military service; also why the British authorities had shrugged aside his political record and issued the work permit.

'Positions held ... Assistant to Professor Naumann at the Charlottenburg Institute 1940 ... Senior chemist at Saalberg research centre 1944 ...'

Yes, Charles had some reason to believe that the pollution had been deliberate and the organism a man-made mutant. Mark turned a page and his heartbeats quickened as he read a synopsis of Graebe's trial before the war crimes tribunal.

Allied Intelligence had suspected – only suspected – that research on biological warfare might have been carried out at Saalberg and Polish prisoners of war used as experimental subjects. But in 1945 the R.A.F. had completely obliterated the establishment, every shred of evidence was destroyed, and Hans Graebe, who had been on compassionate leave to attend his father's funeral when the bombing occurred, was the only survivor. During the tribunal he had freely admitted that the centre was under direct control of the S S., but claimed that he and his colleagues had been working on nerve gases. No biological research had been carried out and no experiments on human beings had ever taken place. Without records – and not a single witness to refute him – his acquittal had been a matter of course.

'Convinced, Mark?' Kirk came back into the room. 'As you know, I've always suspected Graebe was a bad hat, and I should have described his career in detail when we first discussed the Linsleat affair. And now there's no doubt at all. Herr Doktor Graebe is a nut-case and he's returned to his old tricks.'

'I'm not completely convinced, Charles.' Mark took a last look at the photograph and closed the folder. 'There's a possibility that you're right, but no more than that. They may have been working on germ warfare at Saalberg, but so are our people at Porton and that does not automatically make them insane or evil. For all I know, Graebe may be a convinced Nazi, but as you once implied yourself, the mad scientist dreaming up a private *Götterdämmerung* is a bit much to swallow.

'Besides, Daniel Ryder was a very shrewd judge of character and he was also half-Jewish. If Graebe had shown signs that he was unstable or had kept his Nazi beliefs, Ryder would never have employed him.

'There's also another reason for rejecting your notion, Charles. If the pollution was deliberate and the causative agent an artificially produced mutant, it could take a hell of a lot of stopping, so what happens to Graebe himself? He'd not only destroy a great many human beings and animals, he might be committing suicide.'

'Maybe he's a suicidal type craving company, Mark, but we'll have the truth out of him soon enough.' Kirk's weariness had vanished and he looked completely sure of himself. 'I've been on the phone to Belfast and, once they have a warrant, the police will take over the chemical factory lock, stock and barrel. Graebe's laboratory and records will be gone through with a fine-tooth comb, and to make sure the search is really thorough I'm flying out there this evening.'

'I wish you luck, Charles, but I think you'll find that Graebe is not a fiend but a dupe. A rash, irresponsible man who made a mistake and refused to admit it. I still believe that some form of protozoa – probably quite an innocent one – found its way into the preparation they were working on, and chance chemical reaction produced a mutant. If that's what the thing is.

'Graebe may have suspected this, but he wanted to keep his precious formula secret and decided to play possum.' While he talked, Mark was listing the antibiotics he would use. Acromycin – Ampicillin – Penicillin – Tetracyclin – finally Genomycin K, the most recent and powerful of them all. If one of those didn't hit the culture, nothing else would.

'No, Charles, forget the crazy scientist planning racial destruction in the ruined cellar. If Graebe was mad, Daniel Ryder would have rumbled him long ago and he'd hardly have risked drinking that effluent.'

'Maybe he had rumbled him, Mark – or started to.' Kirk took a cigar from his breast-pocket. 'Graebe was Ryder's protégé whom he'd appointed against the wishes of his board of directors. If Ryder had suspected that Graebe was not all he appeared, there might have been two reasons why he drank that effluent.

'No, he couldn't have believed that the stuff would harm him. That would be too much to swallow.' The general grinned at the unfortunate phrase. 'But could he have been

reassuring himself, as well as you, by the gesture? If his suspicions were correct, he had been a fool to appoint Graebe
and his fellow directors were right. Ryder wasn't a man who
would like to be proved gullible or foolish, so was he trying to
drive doubts from his own mind? To demonstrate to himself
that Graebe was completely loyal and his appointment was a
wise choice?

'Sorry, this must sound pretty illogical, but I'm just thinking aloud . . . trying to form a theory . . . to work out a possible
reason why . . .' He stood frowning at the cigar in his maimed
hand. 'But there's something else that might fit in. You told
me that that fellow with the odd name, Bragshaw, thought
Ryder's fall was not an accident, and my guess is that he's right.

'Suppose Graebe is a mental case . . . suppose he realized
that Ryder had started to get wise to him . . . suppose he also
knew how Ryder's tenants felt towards him.' Kirk cut the end
of his cigar with agonizing slowness.

'I know what I'd have done in Graebe's shoes, Mark. I'd
have gone to Treflys and paid some disgruntled Welshmen to
shove him over that mountain.'

Chapter Thirteen

Ryder's safe contained a list of names; among them were
Graebe and Turner, and the date beside Turner was the day
Tania lost her baby. Mark listened to her voice on the telephone. Tania had rung him from the Rose and Leek and he
could hear a murmur of conversation from the bars.

'This man Demchinsky, a Soviet official whom Ryder could
hardly have known socially, addressed him as "My very dear
friend and comrade"? It's certainly curious, darling, and I'd
like to know what was so special about those airspeed indicators. Why should Ryder have changed to a Russian instrument
when Bragshaw and the other directors were quite satisfied

with the British model? Also, what persuaded Demchinsky to defect?' Mark was puzzled and disturbed by Tania's information, but he had too many other problems to give it his absolute attention. He was in an office adjoining the laboratory, and behind the partition Paul Johnston would have played their last card and treated the cultures with Genomycin K. An hour had passed since they went over to the offensive, and so far an impressive list of defeats had been chalked up. Acromycin – Ampicillin – Penicillin – Tetracyclin: all had failed. If the Genomycin produced no reaction, the war might be lost. Could no antibiotic kill the monster that D.R. effluent had spawned?

'Something stinks to high heaven, darling. Did you tell Meg what you found?'

'No, Mark.' Tania stood aside to let three men pass down the passage from the public bar. They nodded civilly to her, but their faces were sullen. 'I don't think Meg would be very pleased to hear that I'd opened the safe without asking her and that's why I came out to phone you. But I'm pretty sure that Ryder told her precious little about his affairs, and Meg's completely at sea. She's also a bag of nerves at the moment.' Tania remembered how Megan's smile had turned to cold fury when she motioned Rushton to the door. 'Mark, Charles Kirk could tell us about the Demchinsky business. Is he with you?'

'Kirk's gone to Ireland, I'm afraid. The old boy's got a notion that the Linsleat pollution was deliberate, and they're going to tear Ryder's factory apart.' A silly notion, Mark had thought till a few minutes ago. *Genus Linsleatensis,* as he had begun to call the organism, was no man-made mutant, but a freak produced by nature and chance chemical reaction. But now the failure of the antibiotics and Tania's information had shaken his confidence, and he wasn't sure about anything.

Graebe . . . Demchinsky . . . Turner. Three names on a list. The chief scientist at a wartime research unit in Germany; a

Russian engineer who had been shot down on the Berlin Wall; a salesman who had lost control of his car when one of Ryder's aircraft passed overhead – a salesman who had been given a job by Ryder. What was the connection between them? Why had Ryder referred to them as 'friends and comrades'?

'Tania, though Kirk's not here, you might get through to the *Globe* and see what John Forest knows about Demchinsky. The fellow has his finger in every pie, if it has news value and is dirty enough.' He looked up as Paul Johnston came in from the laboratory. 'No, darling, I daren't talk to Forest myself. He'd try to pump me, and this business must be kept dark for the time being.

'Just a moment, Paul.' Mark frowned at Johnston who was nodding impatiently towards the doorway. When one antibiotic after another failed to destroy the cultures, the boy's face had become drawn and anxious, but now it wore a slightly smug expression. 'Speak to John Forest, Tania, and find out all you can about Demchinsky.

'For Christ's sake stop that.' Johnston was standing beside him and motioning him to finish the conversation, but though Mark snapped, he was eager to know what had caused his excitement. 'I must go now, but ring me back as soon as you've had a word with Forest, darling. Goodbye for the present.

'Have you forgotten your manners, Paul?' He slammed down the phone. 'I presume that the Genomycin has worked, as we thought it might in time, but there's no need to be bloody rude.'

'Sorry to interrupt you, Sir Marcus.' Johnston strutted pompously into the laboratory as if their roles had been reversed. 'No, Genomycin has had no more effect than any of the other antibiotics you selected, but something else has.' He waved a lordly hand towards a microscope. 'Because of the lack of success, I tried a hunch of my own and added Histocyn VI to one of the cultures.'

'Then you'd better go back to college, son.' Mark might be

fond of Paul Johnston, but he felt like delivering a kick up his backside. 'If Genomycin couldn't hit the blighters, what the hell do you think Histocyn can do? Give 'em a love-pat?'

'Perhaps you would care to see for yourself, sir.' He bowed at a microscope like a conjuror about to reveal the chicken. 'I've got a specimen ready for your inspection.'

'Thank you. If you insist on wasting my time, I suppose I must oblige.' Mark scowled over the instrument and then gave a low whistle of astonishment. The microbes were dead, and it was unlikely that the methylene-blue dye had killed them. Their crab-like bodies had died before the stain was administered, and they lay shrunken and withered on the slide.

'Well . . . well, Paul. It appears that I owe you . . .' He broke off abruptly. He'd apologized to old Dr Travers about the effluent, but he wasn't going to apologize to a pompous youth of twenty-two, however lucky his hunch. 'Yes, the culture's been destroyed right enough, but I can't for the life of me see how Histocyn could be responsible.'

'The proof of the pudding's in the eating, as they say, sir.' The boy's conceit was insufferable and he reminded Mark of an intolerant lecturer addressing a slow-witted student. 'Would you like another demonstration?'

'I damn well would. Prepare two slides from the same saucer; treat one specimen with Histocyn and don't interfere with the other. And no stain this time. We'll try a hanging droplet system.' Mark started to adjust a big German instrument while Paul got to work. He just couldn't understand how the drug the boy had used had halted the organism. Histocyn was a very early antibiotic, discovered shortly after Penicillin, and it was only prescribed for minor sinus infections nowadays. Comparing its powers with Genomycin was like racing a London taxi against a Jaguar.

'Here goes.' The untreated slide was in position and Mark prayed that Johnston was right as he bent forward. He didn't give a damn if his arrogant assistant had succeeded where he had failed. He just wanted to know how those tiny enemies could be destroyed, and they had tried almost every method without success. If Paul was wrong and an epidemic started, they would have no defence against it.

And Paul was wrong ... quite wrong. Though light refracted by drops of liquid produced a poorer image than an aniline dye, the evidence was clear enough. The things were dead, but no stain or antibiotic had killed them. Like the others, they lay withered and harmless before his eyes and the threat of pandemic was over.

'Sorry, Paul. Histocyn wasn't our saviour, but not to worry. There's nothing to worry about any more.' He straightened and thumped Johnston's shoulder triumphantly. 'As you know, our friends have an energetic life-cycle, and that's what put paid to them. They either worked themselves into the grave or died of premature old age.'

*   *   *

'Demchinsky ... Vladimir Ivanovich Demchinsky. You want to know what really happened to him and you've come to the right person, Tania.' John Forest was in his office at the *London Daily Globe,* but the line was so clear and his enunciation so perfect that he might have been standing beside her in the pub passage.

'It was I who unearthed the story, as it happens, but the fruits of my labour were transferred to the *Weekend Star* because our masters considered the material to be Sunday reading. Such a pity. The *Star* newsroom is occupied by a most untalented collection of hacks and as usual they botched and garbled everything.' Forest was an immensely fat man and his voice matched his appearance. The words flowed from the receiver like drops of liquid lard.

'Well, my dear, we are old friends and I am at your disposal, but fair's fair. If you want to hear the full facts about Demchinsky, we must strike a bargain. I'm very curious to know why your good gentleman cut short his holiday and hurried back to Central Laboratories. You can rely on my discretion, of course.'

'I'm sure I can, John, but I just don't know what Mark's up to.' Though Tania liked John Forest, the lie came easily because she didn't trust him an inch. News came before friendship where he was concerned, profit outweighed promises and, as one of his colleagues had remarked, 'When you shake hands with Fat John, watch that his free hand's not pinching your wallet.' 'But if you'll fill me in on Demchinsky, I'll see that Mark talks to you when he can.'

'When he can ... if he wants to ... should he be allowed to.' The reporter's lips clicked petulantly. 'Not much of a bargain, Tania, but I suppose I'll have to play ball with you. The Demchinsky's story's dead anyway, the editors killed it. Your pal Kirk probably saw to that, which makes me wonder why you didn't go to him for the information.'

'Because I couldn't get hold of him, John.' The door of the saloon bar was open and she could see a group of men ranged around the counter. Like those who had passed her while she spoke to Mark, they looked sullen and resentful. Probably the news that Rushton was to continue his survey had reached the village. 'Kirk's gone to Ireland.'

'Indeed!' Tania could picture Forest's smile and she cursed herself for blurting out the information. 'Is more trouble in store for that land of saints and heroes?

'Thank you for a small news item, my dear, and now to the case of Demchinsky. A very odd case indeed. An associate of mine at the Tass agency drinks rather more than is wise, and in his cups he told me that Demchinsky was the very last person one would have considered a potential defector. Apparently the K.G.B. were flabbergasted, and it was quite by chance and at the last moment that the Berlin police discovered the escape plan.' The line gurgled like a waste-pipe. Either Forest had belched or he had found something amusing. 'Yes, without bad luck Comrade Demchinsky would be alive and with us now. To give the story a bit more spice, I hinted that our agents were incompetent. How Kirk loved me for that.'

'You say that the K.G.B. were taken unawares because they had complete trust in Demchinsky, John?' Tania knew the kind of security checks the man would have had to pass before leaving Russia. Defecting writers and ballet dancers could be shrugged aside but a scientist was quite another matter.

'According to my Tass pal they were, and they passed the matter off by saying that Demchinsky had had a sudden brainstorm and lost his reason.' A chair creaked as Forest edged his massive buttocks into a more comfortable position. 'A quiet chap, apparently; unmarried, no close friends and not too popular with his colleagues. Keep-yourself-to-yourself type, but nothing to suggest that he was politically unreliable. My guess is that the K.G.B. were right about a brainstorm and his deathbed scene proves it.

'Demchinsky had five bullets in him when he fell over the Wall, and he was out cold and an obvious goner before they got him to hospital. So our chaps decided to wake him up, bless their kindly hearts.' The thick voice became guarded. 'The *Star* couldn't print this, Tania, and I'll ask you to keep what I'm going to say to yourself. We don't want any trouble from the Official Secrets Act, do we, my dear?

'Demchinsky was one of the Soviet Union's top aviation experts with important information to dispose of, so the poor sod got a shot of Pentothal, the truth drug, to jog his memory. When he responded, they told him that there was no chance of saving his life and he might as well spill the beans before he croaked. You may not believe that of Kirk's brave boys, but it's gospel, and I paid a nursing sister fifty quid for the story.

'You'll never guess Demchinsky's reaction, though. He laughed at 'em . . . told 'em they were a batch of fools and liars and he wasn't going to die.' Forest's throaty chuckle drove home the joke. 'Oh, he died all right. He was riddled with bullet holes and he quite literally split his sides laughing. But though he was raving, I'd like to have seen the bastards' faces when they heard his last words.

'Demchinsky said he was immortal . . . that a bullet capable of killing him would need enough velocity to punch a hole through the centre of the bloody earth.'

* * *

'Wunderschön, dear comrade. This must be it – the chance lead that we have been praying for. I can feel it in my bones, and soon we will be on the way home.' The man from Linsleat was also telephoning. 'God really does work in a mysterious way, doesn't He? At the very moment things become awkward here, your revelation takes place.

'Don't worry, my friend. The police are on the premises, but there is no charge on which they can hold me and I shall be with you to keep the appointment.' He fondled a fountain-pen while he spoke, running his fingers lovingly over the plastic barrel as if it was made of gold or precious stone.

'What can they find, anyway? The Ministry inspectors were quite satisfied and we have nothing to hide. The trials are over and the only evidence is on my person.' The pen twirled and glittered between his fingers. 'As you know, the first two strains were weaklings: mere prototypes which I knew would fail and released experimentally. Such a nuisance that those fishermen were affected, but the evidence will have vanished by now.' He looked at his watch. 'The earlier life-cycles were limited to twenty generations of five hours' duration each, and then the race perished.

'But my final creation will live just as long as our purpose requires. One single culture can populate the earth, and like us it is waiting for the day.' He raised the pen to his lips, blew a kiss and then clipped it carefully into his pocket.

'But I had better ring off and get started. Let us hope that my plane is one of our own. That will be a prophetic coincidence.' He reached for an airline timetable above his desk. 'Goodbye for the present, my dear friend.'

He replaced the phone and looked towards the window. There had been trouble in Linsleat New Town during the early hours of the morning and a Protestant-owned warehouse had been set alight. The fires were out, but the authorities were expecting more violence tonight and barricades had been erected. The man enjoyed the thought of trouble – though this was only a pin-prick, a muted overture to the symphony that was coming. All the same, he hoped he wouldn't be delayed on his way to the airport.

The Day ... D-Day ... Der Tag ... The Day of Judgment, he thought, as he put on his hat and coat and once again checked to see that the pen was securely in position. But what was the other day? The day they had substituted for SOS?

'Da-da ... der-da ... da-der-da-da.' He mouthed the Morse impulses and winced as a sudden pain racked his stomach. Marcus Levin had considered that no man, however wicked or insane, would plan mass destruction at the risk of his own life. But he was wrong. Hans Graebe would be glad to be rid of his body because it was dying of cancer.

'Da-der-da-da ...' In spite of the agony of his tumours, Graebe smiled at the call sign of disaster. 'Mayday,' he said to the room he was leaving for the last time. 'Mayday ... Heyday ... God send Payday.'

Chapter Fourteen

''Mid the field lie dead and dying ... Friend and foe together lying.' Mark sang to keep himself awake, as a dual carriageway opened up and he swung the car past a crawling lorry that had been holding him back. 'Wounded men for mercy crying with their parting breath.'

Eighty miles an hour, ninety, a ton-up – as the motorcycle maniacs call a hundred. He was getting on, he was well into Wales and soon the lights of Rydercraft's Llancir factory would appear on the horizon. Soon he would know if he had set out on a wild-goose chase . . . soon Cedric Bragshaw would demonstrate the workings of a Soviet-made instrument and prove him a fool. He was almost sure that he was wrong, and how he hoped he was! The notion that had occurred to him after Tania had reported her conversation with Forest was both repulsive and ludicrous: a nightmare beyond the bounds of credibility. But for his peace of mind he had had to telephone Bragshaw and ask for proof.

All the same, if he was not wrong . . . if his horrible suspicion proved true . . . ''Mid the field lie dead and dying.' He repeated the line as he slowed for a roundabout. One strain of *Genus Linsleatensis* was dead. It had withered from exhaustion and old age, but before it died he and Paul Johnston had been powerless against it, and they had never seen germ cultures grow so rapidly or in such varied conditions. They had produced them in distilled water, saline solution, on blotting paper and in temperatures ranging from eighty degrees centigrade to freezing point. The rate of multiplication was fantastic and if a second strain existed – a creature with lessened activity and a longer life-cycle – it would be virtually unstoppable. A great number of human beings would be dead or dying if they stood in the path of that advance.

A Russian defector who claimed immortality, a German chemist who had been acquitted of war crimes, the driver of a car who had been startled by aircraft noise, an experienced mountaineer who fell on Allt y Cnicht. They, and the things that had swarmed so unnaturally in the culture saucers, had given him his nonsensical fears, and in a few minutes Cedric Bragshaw would be laughing at his expense. The Linsleat phenomenon was an accidental freak; it had to be. Not even the deranged Nazi scientist of Kirk's imagination could have produced such a monster.

Very, very soon now. The town of Llancir lay straight ahead, and there was a signpost coming up. 'RYDERCRAFT AVI-ATION LTD. PRIVATE ROAD. NO UNAUTHORIZED VEHICLES.' But clearer than any signpost was the sobbing, pulsing howl of a Skyrider revving up on the airstrip. Mark drove up a side road on the right and halted at a barrier.

'Sir Marcus Levin?' He had not shaved for a long time and the man at the gate eyed him critically. 'Yes, Mr Bragshaw's expecting you, but may I have some identification, please?' He inspected Mark's driving licence and grimaced as the Skyrider took off, its jets making speech almost impossible. 'Noisy bastards, aren't they, Sir Marcus?' He handed back the licence. 'You'll find Mr Bragshaw in Number 5 Workshop. That's behind the Admin block. First right, second left and first left again, sir.'

'Thank you.' Mark drove on, past hangars and factory buildings, canteens and offices. Daniel Ryder had played the generous squire to the people of Treflys and he appeared to have been a benevolent employer as well. The buildings were laid out like a garden suburb around lawns and flowerbeds, there was a sports ground and a recreation hall alongside the airstrip, and the whole complex had an atmosphere of con-tented efficiency. He had heard that Rydercraft's production had never once been halted by an unofficial strike, and cer-tainly production was in full progress this evening. Almost every building was alight, the car parks were full and there was a steady hum of machinery.

'WORKSHOP 5.' He pulled up before a small, windowless block of concrete resembling a military bunker, and walked over to its single doorway, which had an electric sign pro-claiming 'NO ADMITTANCE' above the lintel. As he rang the bell, he recalled Bragshaw's disbelief on the telephone, and he expected to receive more scorn in a moment or two. Bragshaw considered the new airspeed indicators a needless expense, but he was certain there could be nothing sinister about them. How Mark prayed that that was the case!

'Ah, it's you.' The sign had gone out, the door opened and Bragshaw nodded to him, but there was no contempt in his face. It was strangely without expression and he looked physically unwell.

'Come in, Mark.' He bolted the door behind them and limped over to a workbench. The snake bite was still troubling him and he leaned heavily on a stick. 'Sorry if I was a bit brusque on the phone, but quite frankly I thought you were barmy and I was up to my ears in work. Only just started to look into the matter and I have to eat my words, it seems.'

'You mean I was right?' Mark looked at the pieces of dismembered apparatus strewn on the bench. 'There *is* something wrong with the airspeed indicators that Ryder ordered?'

'Depends on the designer's point of view, old boy. What he intended the apparatus to do. I'd say that hellish would be a better description than wrong.' Bragshaw pulled on a pair of thick rubber gloves and pointed at a tapered cylinder in a vice. 'The actual indicator unit is quite orthodox, but this is the Pitot head: the activating mechanism which is fitted outside the fuselage and operates the dial. An over-complicated bag of tricks, but efficient enough. That cylinder contains a plastic ball filled with liquid and connected to this tube.'

'Liquid?' His hunch was materializing and Mark felt a stab of nausea. 'What liquid?'

'Should be light mineral oil, according to the specification, but it isn't, and my guess is that the Russians have planned some very nasty industrial sabotage which would have gone undetected if you hadn't given me the tip.

'No, don't touch anything with your bare hands.' He raised his voice as Marcus reached out at the tube which had been sawn off two inches from the base of the cylinder. 'I'll tell you why in a moment, but first you'd better understand how the apparatus works.

'In flight, air squeezes the ball against the sides of the cylinder, the liquid is compressed and the tube forced back to activate an electrical resistance connected to the instrument on the flight deck. Same principle as those things kids used to blow in your face at Christmas parties. All quite straightforward, but in this case the liquid happens to be sulphuric acid.'

'Acid!' That was almost the last thing Mark had expected, and it came as a relief. 'Only acid?'

'*Only*, indeed. Can't you understand what this means, old boy?' Bragshaw picked up a steel probe. 'These instruments were to be fitted to all the new aircraft, and also to those that come in for a works service. After a predetermined period, our fleet would have been grounded by instrument failures and the Russian salesmen given a field-day. They've been trying to compete against us for years, but their blasted TUK 108 can't hold a candle to the Skyrider. What a con trick! How did the bastards get Dan Ryder to fall for it?' Bragshaw eased the probe into the cylinder, edging the plastic tube forward as he did so.

'Got you.' The thing lay on the bench: a flexible black capsule about the size of a tangerine. 'And there appears to be something inside.' Bragshaw squeezed the ball gingerly. 'Put on that spare pair of gloves and feel for yourself.'

'There's an inner container all right.' Mark's nausea returned as he fingered the casing. 'It feels rather like a cigarette-lighter cartridge. And the ball itself has been cut open and resealed at some time; probably with an epoxy resin.' He pointed to a narrow line. 'If the plastic was resistant to acid and the cartridge was metal . . .'

'Let's see exactly what it is.' Bragshaw took the ball from him and opened a penknife. Though flexible, the material was tough and for a moment his blade made no impression. He turned to get a better purchase and then winced with pain as his poisoned ankle took his weight. The knife slipped.

'Down ... get down.' The capsule had burst like a blister and for a split second Mark saw the thing it contained, saw the point of the knife dig into metal; he clutched Bragshaw's shoulder and threw himself sideways. Light blinded them, sound hammered their eardrums, burning gases roared above them as they reached the floor.

* * *

'Bastards ... bloody murderous Bolshevik swine.' Bragshaw pulled himself to his feet. The explosion had not been severe, nobody outside the room appeared to have heard it, but without the bench shielding them he and Mark would have been dead.

'Acid and metal: a simple timing-device that a child could have designed. The plastic would have a high resistance to acid, and the inner container would dissolve more quickly. And in the container you put some substance like Teledyne.' He stood scowling at the burn-mark on the bench as if unable to believe his eyes. 'Yes, Teledyne would fit the bill nicely. You can heat it, and hammer it, and fire detonators into it, and nothing happens. But introduce the stuff to any form of acid and up she goes.

'Jesus! If that Pitot head had exploded against an aircraft flying at operational altitudes, it would have punched a hole in the fuselage and decompressed her.' Bragshaw's face was pouring with sweat and his hands trembled convulsively. 'I thought they only wanted to ground the planes, but this is mass murder.

'Why, Mark? Why should the Russians try to do such a thing? Hell, they operate quite a few Skyriders themselves.'

'Almost every country in the world operates a fleet, Cedric, and it wasn't the Russians who fitted that bomb, but just one

Russian, one individual, working on his own.' Mark pondered Demchinsky's dying words and he tried to remember a saying of Sherlock Holmes. 'Consider everything and reject everything that is not fact. What remains must be the truth, however unlikely it appears.' Yes, the maxim went something like that and, though his own notion was unlikely, the facts were clicking together. He thought of what Tania had told him, he thought of what he had seen in the laboratory, and he looked up at the roof. All over the world Ryder's aircraft were circling the skies with their passengers and cargoes, and one day some rather unorthodox cargoes might be loaded aboard them. Goods to be released by high explosives provided by a man who believed in immortality. Pandora's boxes full of mischief to trouble the earth.

'Thanks, Cedric.' Bragshaw had held out a flask and he took a long pull at the brandy. 'You told me on the phone that no planes would be fitted with the new airspeed indicators till next week, and obviously the bombs will have been timed to go off much later than that. Those in store will be quite safe, so if you're feeling all right, let's get off to Treflys.'

'Treflys? Are you mad, old boy?' Bragshaw goggled at him. 'Granted you put me wise, but what's Treflys got to do with it? The first thing is to get on to the police and the security people and have this filthy business sorted out.'

'No, that's the second thing. Those units were intended to do much more than destroy a few aircraft and our first job is to talk to the man who ordered them from Russia.' Mark handed back the flask, smiling at Bragshaw's bewilderment. 'That's right, I mean Daniel Ryder. He may be dead, but my guess is that he won't lie down.'

Chapter Fifteen

'. . . Our ghosts and monsters are banished. Grendel's dam is dead, the Plague Maiden no longer rides a corpse through the German forests . . .' Tania was in her bedroom at the manor house reading *The Watcher of the Hills* and she had turned back to check a passage. Each version of the legend differed in detail. In all of them, Daran himself most probably survived ritual stoning and was buried alive, but the fate of his followers varied considerably. Their lifeless bodies had been thrown over the mountain; they had been transformed into birds and flown away; their spirits had left them and possessed their persecutors.

Here was that reference from the Nantlynn Abbey rolls. 'The Gaels did feast and rejoice at their victory, but this triumph was short-lived. During the night a number of their people, the exact number of those they had slain, fell sick in mind. As our Lord did later impose upon the swine of Gadara, the unclean spirits of the dead entered into them and they were overcome. To prevent this malady infecting the entire race, their fellows did renounce them. Father turned away son, mother her daughter, husband and wife did curse their partner and the afflicted ones were driven away to walk the land alone.'

A fissure on the mountain had persuaded Judge Roberts that the story was based on fact, but why were Rushton and his party so convinced, and why was Meg terrified of what they might discover? As Bragshaw said, she might be a peasant under the skin but she was also a product of Roedean, a Swiss finishing school and Oxford. Above all, what did Rushton expect to find if Travers gave him the judge's instructions?

Tania could not credit any super-race or supernatural influences, but there must be some germ of truth in the story.

A *germ* of truth . . . 'Sire Daran and his elden, sicken folke.' A race who were considered to be spreaders of disease. She thought of Mark at work in the laboratory, and then of Demchinsky – a man who had died laughing when the truth drug stimulated his brain cells. Finally of Ryder and Turner. Were all their stories somehow connected, and if she could understand what the connection was, would the germs grow and the truth appear?

Names in a safe, a strange mode of address, a Soviet aircraft instrument, an old man's murder. More germs of truth, waiting to unite and increase perhaps.

'The case for the prosecution has been opened.' Tania looked at the last page of the book. 'In the following chapters I shall present and explain the evidence.' That was the end of the text. At that point the judge had put the work aside, and before he took it up again some person or friend of a person he had sentenced with undue harshness, had crept into the cottage and carried out a hideous revenge. Revenge was the generally accepted motive, but Tania was beginning to have other ideas. Could Roberts have been killed because someone had not wanted the treatise published? Or had he been tortured to make him reveal his findings before the work was finished?

She laid down the little book and opened the curtains. Night had fallen, but the cloud had blown away and the moonlight was as bright as when she had seen Bragshaw carrying Ryder's body along the ridge. Not only the moon lit up the valley: headlights were moving along the road. Two sets of lights, and she saw the vehicles pass the end of the drive. One was a Land Rover, probably belonging to the archaeologists, and the other a big glossy limousine that looked like a Jaguar. She dismissed them from her mind and considered the possibility that some local person had killed the judge – somebody she and Mark knew and were friendly with. Had she shaken a hand that had held the judge's face against the fire bars?

Tania pushed the thought aside and leaned out of the window. The sobbing note of a Skyrider was rising and falling over the hills. Obviously one from Llancir and flying low; but it was odd that she couldn't see any navigation lights.

Flying very low indeed. The engines sounded too close for safety; less than three or four thousand feet, and the pilot would barely clear Allt y Cnicht at that height. She looked anxiously up at the sky and then swung round in astonishment. The noise was not coming from outside but from somewhere in the house itself. She stood listening, not knowing what to think, till silence suddenly returned and then she hurried out of the room.

'Hullo, my dear. I do hope I didn't startle you.' Megan Ryder stood beside the safe in the library. Its door was open and the portable tape-recorder Tania had noticed lay on a table. Meg pressed a button and the aircraft noise was resumed.

'You're a good burglar, Tania.' She switched off the set and smiled. 'But you shouldn't have left the combination lying about.'

'I'm sorry.' Tania saw her diary lying on the top of the safe. 'I should never have opened it without asking you, but while you were out curiosity got the better of me. I can only apologize.'

'My dear girl, there's nothing to apologize for.' Meg laid a friendly hand on her arm. 'I wanted the safe opened and you've saved me a lot of trouble. I'll be grateful to you till my dying day.' She stopped smiling and her manner changed. 'What are you waiting for?' She had swung round and Tania saw Willie Price standing beside the window. 'I've told you exactly what to do, so get on with it.'

'No, Missus . . . not again.' Price's big body was slumped forward and there was an abject whine in his voice. 'Not up there at night . . . not on me own, Missus.'

'Don't be such a coward . . . such a stupid baby, Willie, and above all don't argue with me. You have been given an order, you know what has to be done, so carry out my instructions.' Tania had rarely heard a woman speak more authoritatively, and with a resigned gesture Price stooped and lifted a rucksack from the floor and swung it over his shoulders. For an instant he looked towards Meg as though he was going to plead with her again and then he moved off with the pack swaying on his back.

'Yes, I'm very, very grateful to you, Tania.' Meg watched Willie shambling across the hall to carry out whatever her instructions were, and Tania suddenly understood their relationship. Willie Price had been her lover, but Meg was not a masochist and she had not enjoyed the experience. She had offered herself to Willie to turn a paid servant into a slave: an emotionally bound chattel who would obey any order she delivered.

'Without your help I'd never have known the truth till it was too late, Tania. For years I'd suspected that the dangers were real . . . that they were coming closer, but it took you and my dear husband to bring the warnings home to me.' The safe was empty, Meg had piled its contents on the table and Tania saw something she had missed. An over-exposed photograph, probably taken with a flash-bulb. The background was formless, but along it ran a line of marks very similar to those she had seen in Ryder's exercise-book.

'Suspicions . . . unformed fears, my dear. That was all I had to go on till Dan lost his temper and you opened the safe for me.' Meg pointed at the photograph Tania was looking at and her voice carried the complete conviction of the paranoiac. 'I know what those symbols are, I know why Dan brought Rushton here, I know why he gave a home to those wretched dropouts. Above all, I know what this means.'

She turned on the tape-recorder again and once more the sound of a Skyrider pulsed from the speaker; but Tania hardly heard it, because another extract from Judge Roberts's book was running through her mind. '. . . they could not kill the man-beast. Even when his body was broken in the six places that prophecy required did Daran rise up and cry out to his fellows in their ancient language . . .' Stones had broken Ryder's body as well as Daran's and in the same number of places. His skull and rib-cage, his arms and legs had been shattered.

'Clever Tania Levin.' Meg switched off the recording. 'Once this is over we are going to be such good friends, you and I. You not only opened the safe for me, but you discovered that the judge told George Travers where he found those carvings.' She bent forward over the photograph. 'Then you were even cleverer. You told Rushton what George knew, and George is not a determined man like the old judge was. He's weak, he's easy-going and he'll talk – he'll blurt out the directions after a time and then . . . then . . .' She raised the photograph and her voice changed again. It became harsh and brittle as though a very old woman was speaking. 'Can you guess what these signs mean, my dear? Shall I explain the exact nature of evil to you?'

'In a moment, but tell me something first.' There was a thin line of foam running between Megan's lips and Tania sensed she was on the fringe of hysteria. 'Did you kill your husband?'

'I kill Dan?' Tania had expected a strong reaction, but quite the opposite happened. Meg's voice returned to normal and she appeared completely calm once more. 'What a question to ask, Tania. I thought we were friends, so surely you don't imagine I would soil my hands with murder?' She looked saddened by the suggestion, but not at all angry. 'Of course I didn't kill Dan. Willie killed him.'

*   *   *

'It's gotter-be-done, gotter-be-done, gotter-be-done.' Willie

Price muttered to keep himself company while he pedalled his bicycle along the lane.

'It's gotter-be-done because Missus says so.' His eyes swept the horizon. There were the lights of Treflys looking friendly and secure over his left shoulder; there was the sea just visible through the trees; there, looming high above him, was his destination – the thing he hated. Allt y Cnicht, the Hill of the Knight, the Mountain of Daran. How he dreaded going there on his own.

'But it's gotter-be-done.' The words gave him comfort as his feet urged the cycle up the slope. He shouldn't be frightened; this was the third time that he'd made the journey and nothing had happened to him. The first time had been the worst, naturally, and all because of that bloody Ryder.

Willie flushed angrily and his feet pounded harder on the pedals. Ryder had shouted at him to stop the car and then he'd got out and dragged Missus after him. Willie remembered how the swine had looked around to see there was nobody in sight, and then his hands had shot out, tearing her blouse, battering her wonderful body. How could the fool have dared to strike a goddess?

'You must know, Meg. You must have some clue . . . some vague idea where the place is, and you're going to point it out to me.' Ryder's left hand had made Willie think of a talon as it clutched her throat, and again and again his right had slammed out at her. 'No, better than that, you bitch. You're going to take me there. We're going up that mountain together; here and now, my dear, devoted wife.' He'd been so intent that he never saw Willie leap from the driving-seat, and he crumpled at the first blow.

'Kill him, Willie. Kill him for me – for all of us.' Missus had pulled open the torn blouse and stood with her breasts rose-red in the setting sun. 'You've always wanted me, haven't you, Willie? I've known that for years, and you'll get your wish granted if you earn it. Kill the bastard, Willie.

'Not like that.' He had knelt down to strangle Ryder, but she tugged his arm and pointed at a dry-stone wall. 'You know how the story says it should be done. Your parents and grand-parents must have told you. Kill him properly.' She had lifted a coping-stone from the wall and held it out to him.

He hadn't liked what followed. He hadn't liked the way Ryder's bones had crunched, or the moaning, crooning sounds he kept making till a blow on the skull silenced him. But the actual killing had not troubled Willie as much as the journey up the mountain. Every boulder, every shadow seemed an enemy, and when he had laid the body in the stream and sent the scree down on top of it, the falling rocks sounded like voices cursing him.

But when it was all over and he got back to the manor house, Missus had kept her promise. Pride and love drove out Willie's fears as he pedalled on. That foreign woman, Lady Levin, thought he'd been rough with Missus, that he was responsible for the bruises Ryder'd given her; he'd seen it in her expression. But how wrong she was. He'd been so gentle, so full of love and awe, and he'd approached Missus like the goddess he knew her to be. His woman – his mistress in every sense of the word. No danger, no task was too great when she gave the order.

The lane turned a shoulder of the hill and started to slope downwards. Willie rested his feet on the pedals and looked up at the cliffs above him. The contents of his rucksack jingled reassuringly while he coasted along, and he repeated the refrain 'Gotter-be-done, gotter-be-done . . .'

*   *   *

'That's why I had to reward Willie, Tania. The reason for that sordid scene you witnessed.' Megan's hands fluttered around the things she had taken from the safe. Ledgers and files, the photograph and the tape-recorder, a paper-knife and the exercise-book filled with the curious symbols and lists of names, the specification of a Soviet-built airspeed indicator. To Tania they had suddenly become completely unimportant. Everything she had heard from Mark and John Forest had slipped from her mind. She had stopped theorizing and all she could think about was a myth: a legend that had been passed down through the generations to drive men and women mad.

Religion is the opium of the People. She had been made to repeat that parrot-wise when she was a child, but since living in England she had come to consider Karl Marx a dull bigot and had started to take an interest in the occult. But Meg's fluttering hands and crazed confession told her that the slogan was true. Religion and the supernatural were drugs: mental poisons to kill reason and create insanity.

There was no doubt that Meg was mad, but not because she had ordered her husband's death. The *way* it had been done proved her mania. The old judge had lost his reason too, according to George Travers, and probably Ryder had gone the same way. How many other minds had the story of Daran destroyed?

'What a fool Dan was, Tania.' Meg pulled up a sleeve to show the bruises on her arm. 'He might have known that Willie would kill him if he laid a hand on me, but I suppose that scene in the pub made him reckless. George Travers and Emrys had made it clear that Rushton would get no help from the local people, and Dan got it into his head that I might know the way and would lead him there if I did. He hit me, Tania. When I told him that no one knew – that the knowledge was lost and had been lost for centuries – he thought I was lying and he just kept hitting – hitting – hitting me till Willie reached him.' Meg sniggered at the bruises.

'But the knowledge isn't lost, is it? You found that out, Tania. The judge told George Travers where the thing is hidden, didn't he? And though the judge kept his secret, George isn't a strong-minded man like him. George'll talk all right, he'll have talked already, and the last act is going to start.' Meg looked out through the window. There was an unusual amount of traffic about and Tania saw more car lights moving along the road. 'Don't you find the prospect rather exciting, Tania? You and I are going to watch the end of a play that started three thousand years ago.

'And Willie Price, a simpleton, is to be our leading man.' Her gaze swept over the slopes of Allt y Cnicht. 'They're bound to have torches and he'll see them. Willie will watch their progress, study the route they take, and he'll be ready for them. Good, brave Willie. If he hadn't been there to kill Dan, the play might have ended very differently.'

'Why did Willie kill your husband with a rock, Meg?' Tania already knew the answer, but she wanted to find out just how mad Megan was. 'Why did you tell him to break his body in the same way that your ancestors stoned Daran?'

'How clever of you to think of that, Tania. Yes, we really are going to be friends.' She crossed back to the table and stood facing the open door. 'When Dan was dead and Willie started off up the mountain with his corpse, I began to have fears that I had been out of my mind. Quite on the spur of the moment I'd realized how Dan should die ... like a voice in my ear the order had come to me. But afterwards, for a long time afterwards ... right up to the moment I saw the actual evidence to prove what Dan had been ... what he was up to ... where he had got this ...' Her finger ran over the symbols on the photograph.

'But that voice wasn't imaginary, was it? God had spoken to tell me that rituals must always be followed. A silver bullet is needed to kill a werewolf. A stake must be driven through a vampire's heart. Only a stone could destroy the demon that possessed my husband.'

'Your memory's failing, Meg.' Tania felt deep sympathy. The woman was a murderess, but she was also a very sick human being in need of help and understanding of skilled professional treatment. But could any treatment free her from the obsession that the man she had killed was the reincarnation of someone who had died thirty centuries ago? Was there a chance that the legend itself might jerk her back to reality? 'Daran was stoned ritually, but he did not die, Meg. Every version of the story agrees on that. He was alive when your people buried him.'

'What . . . just what . . . ?' Though Meg had been speaking strangely, her voice had remained rational, but now it rose to a scream and the last vestige of sanity seemed to have left her. 'You . . . you . . . How dare you?' She edged round the table and snatched up the paper-knife. Its blade was a full nine inches long and Tania prepared to meet the attack. A sidestep, an ankle kick, and her hands on the wrist and arm.

'You . . . you . . . you . . .' Megan moved slowly forwards with the knife raised and her eyes glowing as though there were light bulbs behind them. Tania braced herself and then swung round, realizing that self-defence was unnecessary. The knife was not intended for her, and even if it had been, a Sir Galahad had arrived to protect her.

When she had last seen the man, he had been dragging his way pathetically past the Rose and Leek, looking ill and shaky and almost too weak to climb the slope. *One of them hippies – Ryder's blasted drop-outs who disgraces the village.*

But he didn't look a drop-out now, he looked rather like Daniel Ryder. There was no hint of illness in those firm confident steps crossing the hall towards them, and no pathos in his manner. Though still ragged and unkempt, he appeared as self-assured as a high-pressure salesman and his hand did not shake when he raised a revolver and centred it on Meg's forehead.

Chapter Sixteen

'That's an off-beat theory if ever there was, and a hellish nasty one.' Bragshaw was considering what Mark had told him as they drove through the Welsh hills. Considering it very critically indeed, almost contemptuously, and if he had not witnessed the explosion in the workshop, he'd have dismissed it at once.

Levin did put me wise to that airspeed indicator, he thought to himself. But to dash over to Treflys with the intention of making old Travers produce Dan Ryder's body is surely irrational. The fellow's supposed to be brilliant – Nobel Prize winner and all that – but it's often the best brains that crack under strain and he's certainly in a state of stress right now. The car was running down the straight slope towards Treflys and he glanced at Mark's troubled eyes and unshaven chin.

'Yes,' he said at last. 'My medical knowledge may be based on Dr Goodfellow's *Guide to Family Health,* but even I have heard about antibodies, Mark. Our own friendly bugs which guard the system against outsiders. But do you honestly believe that what you've suggested is scientifically possible?'

'Possible, but not probable.' Mark did not bother to stifle a yawn. He had taken two pep pills to keep his mind active, but he felt numb with tiredness and had to ask Bragshaw to drive. He had to keep concentrating, though, and talking over the theory was as good a way as any.

'Hans Graebe worked at a Nazi establishment which was believed to be carrying out research on germ warfare. If that is correct he might have solved the one problem which has always prevented the use of such weapons: self-destruction.

'It's a question of the biter being bit.' Bragshaw had grunted a question and Mark tried to explain in simple terms. 'All nat-ural epidemics die out in time, because our defence mecha-nisms have become programmed to deal with them. But there is no difficulty in artificially producing an invincible biological weapon, and you can do it in two ways: selectively breed one of our age-old enemies, such as *Bacillus pestis,* in varying condi-tions, till its structure and behaviour pattern alter; or encour-age an organism which previously has only preyed on other species to attack human cells. The potato blight and parrot disease can easily be adapted in this way. In either case, our sys-tems would have no defence against such an unconventional invasion and down comes baby, cradle and all.

'But all you've made is a boomerang; a two-edged sword. You can kill your enemies as easily as mowing a field, but what happens if the infection swings back on you? Hitler might have enjoyed handing out mutated bacilli to the Allies, but he wouldn't have wanted a dose himself – to feel a plague bubo throbbing in his own groin.'

'Brrh, you're a cynical sod, old boy.' Bragshaw gave a mock shudder. 'So, the trick is to develop immunity in yourselves: to adapt your antibodies to deal with the bugs you've mutated. That's clear enough, but I just can't follow your overall suspi-cions. You seriously consider that groups of people living in separate parts of the world and with no personal associations might have got together and planned something along these lines. Why . . . what's their motive? How could they have con-tacted each other in the first place?

'But just a moment.' He continued excitedly before Mark could answer. 'I've just remembered something I heard from a pal in the Metropolitan Police. It's a hell of a long time since he told me the story and the details slipped my mind till just now, but it might fit in. You know I said that Dan Ryder didn't bash up his face in a climbing accident. Well, what happened was that he either fell or was pushed out of a tart's bedroom window.' He drove very slowly towards the village.

'It happened in Soho about ten or eleven years back, I think. The case never went to court because Dan refused to prefer charges and you can't blame him for that. It would have made sordid reading in the newspapers.' Dr Travers lived a little way outside Treflys and Bragshaw turned up a side road.

'Dan had been spending the night with a prostitute. Ameera something-or-other her name was, and she had a Bengali ponce who dabbled in fortune-telling. They were deported as illegal immigrants later on, but my rozzer pal said they'd have faced a charge of attempted murder if Dan had co-operated with the police, who were pretty sure that they'd robbed him and then slung him through the window.' Bragshaw parked the car before the doctor's house. Travers appeared to be at home; his motorcycle stood beside the porch, and there was a glimmer of light behind the study curtains.

'Dan's statement was that he had a bad hangover and slipped while he was leaning out to get a breath of fresh air. But he was unconscious for a while, and before he talked the girl and her boy-friend gave a different version.

'Are you listening to me, old chap? This could tie up with your notion.' Mark's face was turned away from him and he was staring at the house and sniffing the air. The window behind the curtain must be open and something more than light was coming from it. 'They said that Dan had been troubled by a recurrent dream, and he went gaga and chucked himself into the street after the Indian tried some mumbo-jumbo experiment to show that he was an avatar, the reincarnation of . . .'

Bragshaw finished the sentence, but Mark did not hear him. He had recognized the smell that was drifting from Travers's study and he was out of the car and running towards the window. He tore aside the curtains and gave a gasp of horror.

As they had thought, Dr George Travers was at home. He was kneeling before an electric fire and he had followed the example of Mr Justice Roberts. His wrists and ankles were roped together, and though the fire had been switched off, the room still stank of burning flesh.

'You're wasting time, Mark.' Bragshaw frowned at his efforts. They had cut the cords and George Travers lay stretched out on a settee, inert and apparently lifeless. He had obviously put up a good fight before being overpowered and the room was a shambles: furniture overturned, books and broken glass littering the floor and the telephone torn from the wall.

'I'm no medico, but I've seen a few stiffs over the years and he's dead.' Bragshaw forced himself to look at the terrible face with its peeling skin and cracked lips. 'Besides, you don't imagine the bastards who did that would leave the poor devil alive to talk about it, do you? Only odd thing is why there was no attempt at concealment. You'd have thought they'd have set the house on fire to destroy any evidence. But I suppose they didn't bother, seeing it was his half-day and his house-keeper wasn't due till tomorrow morning.

'Bastards – unspeakable bastards.' Bragshaw blew his nose to get rid of the tang of burning. 'I'd better leave you and cut along to the police station.'

'Stay where you are and keep quiet, please.' Mark lifted his head from Travers's chest and resumed massaging the heart. The old man certainly seemed to be dead. Shock and agony had stopped his circulation, and the kiss of life had done nothing to revive him. But just now Mark fancied that he had heard a hesitant beat, though he might have been mistaken. Probably the pounding of his own heart had created the illusion. He felt beside himself with rage and loathing for the people who could have done such a thing ... who had tortured a harmless old man, just as the judge had been tortured. He had to move heaven and earth to revive Travers and not merely for the sake of saving his life. If Travers could be made to talk for just a few seconds ...

Was that another beat? He couldn't be certain and Bragshaw was probably right. The monsters who had left Travers bound before the fire would have made quite sure he could tell no tales.

Yet there it was again. A definite movement, and another, though so weak, so very hesitant. The man's life hung on a frayed thread which might snap before he could be hauled to safety.

'Please take over from me, Cedric.' With his hands still at work, Mark leaned sideways to let Bragshaw edge in beside him. 'Do you see how it's done? Fingers spread out, thumbs here, and press hard and steadily.'

'That's it. Good – very good.' He nodded and turned to Travers's medicine cabinet. It was locked, but the glass front had been broken in the struggle and he tugged the doors open.

If ever there was a question of 'Physician heal thyself,' he thought. They had no telephone and no time to send to the hospital for supplies, and Travers's life might depend on the medicines he kept in stock.

Nothing, nothing … nothing of any use at all. Mark searched the cabinet, cursing a health service that discouraged doctors from running their own dispensaries. Aspirin and kaolin, surgical spirit and Vaseline, and on the top shelf a stock of samples sent out by pharmaceutical firms. His fingers ran through the collection. An antihistamine preparation for hay fever, multi-vitamin pills, sleeping-capsules gleaming invitingly, antibiotics. But at last! *Phenocytin*. He felt like a child with temptation laid before him as he pulled out the container. Travers should have got rid of the sample months ago, because the drug had been off the market since last winter and the *Lancet* had published an official condemnation. Phenocytin was an effective treatment for melancholia, but the side-effects – convulsions and abnormal vascular activity – made the preparation too dangerous for general use. All the same, it might be the lever he needed and he thought of what Tania had told him about Demchinsky. The would-be defector lying in a Berlin hospital and opening his eyes when the truth drug took effect. Phenocytin was no truth drug, but it did stimulate the heart. 'Can you feel anything – anything at all?'

'I can't be certain.' Bragshaw looked up from the couch. 'Once or twice there seemed to be a flicker, but nothing now. He's finished, Mark, and I'm damned sure this is all useless.'

'There's still a chance.' Mark had found a syringe and he opened the container and took out two phials. Five grains was the recommended intravenous dose for Phenocytin and anything over eighteen produced fatal convulsions. He broke both phials and drew twelve grains into the syringe. If there was any life present, that amount would provide a temporary spur to Travers's heart, but it might also kill him. He looked at the burned face for a second and made his decision.

'Where does he keep his stethoscope?' The drug had been injected and Mark turned back to the cabinet before remembering how Tania had opened Ryder's safe. As he did so, Bragshaw give a hiss of excitement.

'Good grief, old boy. Yes, something's happening. I can hear a distinct beat now.' He drew aside to let Mark take his place, looking as if he had just witnessed a miracle. 'He's going to pull through?'

'That's too much to hope for, I'm afraid, but he may recover consciousness for a minute or two.' Mark spoke with his ear against Travers's chest. The beats were there all right, and becoming stronger and more frequent. The stimulus had worked, but he dreaded to think what that massive dose of Phenocytin was doing to heart muscles already strained by shock and exhaustion.

'You . . . you, Mark.' George Travers's eyelids were cracked and withered, but miraculously the eyes themselves had escaped and they were widening in recognition. 'Have they gone? Really gone?'

'They've gone, George, and you're quite safe.' The doctor's

voice had been barely audible and Mark craned forward. 'But who were they, George? Why did they do this to you?'

'They, of course, the old . . . old . . .' A long shudder racked his body. 'Thought they were squalid nuisances, drug addicts, layabouts, never guessed the truth till I saw Dan Ryder standing at the door. Another man's . . . another man's clothes, but it was Dan Ryder.'

'Ryder's dead, George.' The pulse was quickening and steadying between Mark's fingers, but probably the brain cells had been deprived of blood for so long that Travers's mind had run down. 'You know he's dead, George. You performed Ryder's autopsy yourself, so who was it who tortured you?'

'Thought Ryder was one of them . . . seemed to recognize the expression . . . general manner . . . way he talked. Looked different, that's all. Got a new home . . . same man under the skin.' The doctor's lips were like pale worms writhing on the burned face. 'Always wondered why Dan Ryder gave those beatniks a home . . . Think I know now. They've returned the kindness . . . they and the others . . . the . . .

'It's coming back, Mark, so listen carefully. They told me everything and you must understand what we're up against . . . must . . . must see that . . .' The pulse was racing now, but the beats were erratic and Mark had no idea how long it could continue.

'I didn't realize who they were at first . . . just knew that I had to keep my promise to the judge. Then suddenly . . . right out of the blue, I saw Ryder's personality behind the boy's eyes, and I knew everything. I realized what evil was, I told them to go to hell, Mark, and they tortured me just as Roberts was tortured. I wouldn't say a word to help them, so they tortured old George Travers who never did anybody any real harm.' He caught a glimpse of his face in the mirror and tears trickled down the ravaged cheeks. 'They held me up against the fire and they explained . . . they told me everything and at last I gave in and showed them where to go. But even then

they didn't release me ... they just walked away and left me
... left me kneeling here.'

'Go on talking, George, I'm still listening.' Travers had
fallen silent, but Mark knew that his suspicions were proving
true, though one major detail was lacking. He also suspected
that the reality might be even worse than anything he had
imagined possible. But there was still a lot to learn. 'Where
exactly did you tell them to go?'

'Up past the crag known as the Knight's Visor. To the cliff
where Mr Roberts found the ...' The heartbeats were faltering, the voice was becoming fainter, Dr Travers had only
seconds left. 'Mark, what are you doing here? Why aren't you
going to help her, for God's sake? You see they won't ... won't
rely on my word alone, because I told them ... right at the
end when the pain was too much to bear and I got so angry, so
bitter, remembering that it was she – she who had sent them
here.

'Forgive me, Mark ... please forgive me.' Weaker and
weaker grew the voice and the heartbeats, and Mark strug-
gled to make out the final statement. 'I said that your pretty
Tania had guessed where the thing they wanted was hidden.'

Chapter Seventeen

'Easy as falling off a log.' Willie Price was past the fence and
he took a pair of bolt-cutters from his rucksack and positioned
their blades against a padlock. A single jerk of his shoulders
sliced through the loop and the second barrier had been overcome. He stepped into the dynamite store and laid his electric
lantern on a bench.

The explosives were stacked along the walls in sixty-pound
boxes, there was a locked cupboard containing detonators
and fuses, and parked in the centre of the building were a
fork-lift truck, a trailer and the small tractor which was used to

help lorries up the hill if there was snow about. Willie ignored
the fork-lift – he didn't need any mechanical assistance to load
up – and manhandled the trailer against the far wall. Then
he crossed to the cupboard, the shafts of the cutters swung
together again, another lock snapped and the last barrier was
down. He turned, checked the fuel gauge on the tractor, and
started to load up the trailer.

Forty cases should do the job. His uncle, who had been a
quarryman, had told him a great deal about blasting operations and Willie considered his plans while he lifted the boxes
aboard. The north face of Allt y Cnicht was not merely loose
and riddled with small caves, it was overhanging and at its
base was a deep cleft. If Missus was right, and of course she
was, *they,* he could only think of them as *they,* would be looking for a place somewhere above the cleft, and that was where
he would be stationed. He had to load up, fit detonators and
a firing plunger and then move out and watch for the lights
creeping along the ridge. Missus had said that Dr Travers
would be leading the way, which was a pity because Willie
liked the doctor. But his own feelings were unimportant; all
that mattered was carrying out Missus's exact orders. 'Get
ready, watch the lights, wait till they have vanished into the
mountain, and allow another ten minutes for good measure.'

After that he could press the plunger and drive evil out
of the valley. Anticipation of the approaching spectacle had
lulled Willie's fears and he considered what would happen
when he drove the plunger home. Forty cases of dynamite,
and an overhang to contain the explosion, should make a fine
mess of old Allt y Cnicht. Clever, clever Missus.

One by one the boxes were piled on to the trailer and Willie
tried to imagine the results of Megan's scheme. The flash, the
roar, and the avalanches that would follow. Missus was the
best woman in the world, she was a goddess – his goddess.
She had planned for everything and nothing could go wrong,
he thought, as he moved over to the tractor. The one thing he

did not think about was what would happen to him when the mountain came down.

*   *   *

'Get on, damn you. You must go faster.' Mark cursed his body as he staggered along the ridge. His breath came in gasps, a steel band appeared to be tightening round his chest, and his thin city shoes slipped and stumbled on the rocks. But somehow he forced himself to keep running, and even while he cursed, he blessed the impulse that had prompted him to take Travers's motorcycle and leave Bragshaw with the car. The people he was following had a long start, but the machine had carried him right up to the foot of the ridge before he had abandoned it.

Tania, Tania my darling. His eyes swept over the mountain. He had been seeing torchlights intermittently since leaving the manor house, but now they had vanished for at least ten minutes and there was nothing to guide him. No movement except the moon and a few clouds drifting above the summit.

'Tania, where are you, Tania?' He remembered how he had shouted her name when he burst into the house, hardly daring to breathe the air for fear that it might contain a reek of burning. Judge Roberts and George Travers had died because they knew where a certain spot on Allt y Cnicht was situated, and the people who had held their bound bodies before a fire believed that his wife had the information.

'Tania . . . Tania.' Again and again he had shouted while he ran from one room to the next, picturing Travers's face seared like bacon under a grill and fighting back an image of what his wife's face might look like if the murderers had found her. People! Murderers! What inept words to use, he had thought. Human beings had not killed Travers and Roberts, men and women were not responsible for the things that had happened at Linsleat and the last pieces of the jigsaw could be fitted together. He was dealing with a completely alien force that had been sleeping for centuries when Daniel Ryder awakened it.

Find Tania, though ... must find Tania. However great the general menace, nothing mattered except that, and she might already have joined the cast of the terrible play that was Ryder's dream-child.

'My darling – my love, what have they done to you?' He had stood swaying in the library doorway, forcing himself to breathe in, not recognizing the smell of cordite at first, and before he moved towards the woman's body on the floor, he had mouthed a prayer, a cry for help which he had last heard spoken by a dying rabbi at Belsen. 'Shema Yisroel ... Adonai Elohenu ...

'Thank you ... thank you, God.' He had turned the face up, and despite shock and pity he could not repress joy. Megan Ryder was dead, but she had not been tortured. Her expression was quite peaceful and the bullet's entry wound in her forehead looked as innocent as a Hindu caste-mark.

He had stood up and leaned against the table, trying to marshal his thoughts. Tania must be with them and a place on the mountain was their goal. A cliff somewhere beyond a crag called the Knight's Visor, but how could he find it? He looked at the things on the table, recalling Tania's description of what the safe contained. An exercise-book with lines of scrawled signs and symbols joined by passages in English. A photograph showing similar symbols which could prove Ryder the old judge's killer. Roberts had probably taken that picture; it showed fragments of writing which had been used three thousand years ago, and the judge had died rather than reveal the place where he had found them.

A tape-recorder. Was it possible that that might help him? Mark pressed the switch, praying to hear some conversation containing a reference ... perhaps Tania's voice repeating what Travers had told her. But only the sound of a Skyrider droned from the speaker and he had turned despairingly towards the window. How vast the hills looked in the gloom, how small was the human body, he had thought, and then hope came surging up and he had run for the door. Lights were moving along the ridge, and with the recorder still throbbing in his hand he had mounted the motorcycle and ridden off.

And now at last, over to the right and emerging from behind a bluff came the lights again. Tiny pinpoints, like glowworms, about five hundred feet above him.

The tape-recorder jolted in Mark's pocket as he ran on. He had no idea what he would do when he reached his quarry, but he knew that they were every man's enemies and their motive destruction. The Linsleat microbes were theirs, the writing Judge Roberts had located was theirs, and an exhaust note reproduced their language: a chant that had been heard on Allt y Cnicht before the Celts came.

Had a conventional aircraft started Daniel Ryder's dream, perhaps? Whatever the case might be, his racial memories were revived and an Indian ponce had shown him what he was. Ryder's human personality must have been revolted, for he had thrown himself from a window to escape destiny. But when he recovered he realized that there was no release, he had accepted what he had to do and planned a way to contact his fellows. Modulated sounds from the sky which Hans Graebe had heard, and Demchinsky and countless others, were his methods – reproductions of a chant, which caused Turner to lose control of his car – call signs to be answered by Rydercraft's questionnaires. The bent crusade could begin, and Graebe had forged the weapons: tiny monsters from which immunity was the only escape; germ cultures to be released from plunging Skyriders after bombs shattered their fuselages.

Mark was positive about those details. He was also fairly sure how the spreaders of sickness had developed immunity in themselves and it had nothing to do with his earlier suspicions. Daniel Ryder's body was dead all right, and if the rocks had not killed it, *Genus Linsleatensis* would have had no difficulty when the time arose. Only one piece was needed to complete the puzzle and he still had no idea what it was. The lights vanished again, the moon was screened by cloud, and Mark considered the problem while he stumbled up through the gloom.

What did the 'friends and comrades' hope to find on the mountain?

★   ★   ★

That was it, and he'd done a right good job. Willie Price stepped down from the tractor and walked away, paying out a coil of wire behind him. The loaded trailer was well under the overhanging cliff, detonators were positioned in two of the dynamite boxes and everything was ready. The exploder, a dynamo with a plunger mechanism to send an electric current leaping down the wire to the detonators, was in his rucksack, and all he had to do was connect up and wait.

The waiting would be the worst part. He settled himself on a clump of heather, fitted the wire to the terminals and screwed in the plunger handle. He could kill the bastards at this moment, he thought, looking up at the line of lights moving high above him. All he had to do was to drive the plunger home. Over a ton of dynamite, contained by that overhang, would bring down the whole north face of Allt y Cnicht and that would be the end of the menace to Treflys valley.

Why shouldn't he do it now? Willie's hand ran longingly over the handle. The lights were approaching the final climb up to the summit and travelling very slowly and erratically: circling and zigzagging over the terrain as if their owners had lost the way. They were just in the right position, though – almost exactly above the trailer – and all that was needed was one good, hard push on the plunger.

No, he had to wait. Missus had told him to do nothing till they had reached their destination and the lights vanished. He had to follow her instructions even if it meant moving the trailer farther along the cliffs. Willie removed his hand and concentrated on studying the lights and remembering what Missus had told him.

He must wait till the lights disappeared and then for another ten minutes after that. Missus had not told him exactly why, but he could guess all right. He knew what they were trying to find; his parents and grandparents had told him the story a hundred times when he was a boy. Killing them was necessary, he had to kill them, but that was not the most important part of his mission. They were just guides to show him where the place was. It was the thing they were looking for that had to be destroyed.

Chapter Eighteen

> Up the airy mountain,
> Down the rushy glen
> We daren't go a-hunting . . .

The verse ran through Tania's head as it had done on the night Ryder's body had been brought down from the mountain, but this time she was not alone. She was standing before a cliff face – she was listening to the thud of hammers – she was watching the creatures she had been ordained to serve.

'For fear of little men.' The phrase was not really appropriate. Some of them could be described as little, but some were heavily built, some tall, some medium-sized. They also varied in other ways: some were dark, others fair or medium-coloured; they were drawn from different age groups, nationalities and walks of life. And with the exception of Hans Graebe's boyish face and sick body, there was nothing particularly distinctive or frightening about their appearance. It was the things they harboured, the mental parasites that had entered and controlled their minds, that inspired terror. The 'friends and comrades' were together again; she had brought the spirits of the old ones up the mountain.

'Yes, it is I, Tania,' Daniel Ryder had said in the library, lowering the gun with which he had just killed his wife, and speaking through the mouth of a young man. 'Megan and Willie Price could not harm an immortal soul and as the good book says, "The voice is Jacob's voice, but the hands are the hands of Esau."' The youthful eyes had twinkled as he stepped aside to let five of his companions file into the room: the Frenchman and the schoolmistress who called at the cottage, another of the archaeologists whom Tania had been briefly introduced to, Professor Rushton and a second inmate of Ryder's hostel, 'one o' them blasted hippies'. But, like his fellow, the hippie did not look ill or indecisive. He looked completely self-confident, and when he spoke to Tania it was in Russian. Vladimir Ivanovich Demchinsky was a man of his word and had fulfilled the boast that he would not die.

None of them could die because, though the actors changed their costumes, the play ran for ever. Rushton had told her this while he unrolled a map on the table beside Meg's body. He looked as much the screen frontiersman as ever and Tania had realized why when Hans Graebe came into the library clicking his heels and bowing like a Prussian officer. Ryder had imitated the country squire, the Frenchman was a parody of Maurice Chevalier. They were all playing parts because their human personalities had withered and they had had to adopt stock-character roles.

Rushton had still spoken benevolently when he described what had been done to George Travers and explained what was required of her. His hands had been gentle when he tied her wrists together, and once again he had delivered a lecture while the Land Rover lurched up the track towards Allt y Cnicht.

'Mankind is not a family group, but a tree,' he had said. 'At the moment it has many branches, but with one exception these must be lopped off, because evolution intends that only a single branch may survive and mature. One great racial force spreading across the earth, climbing to the planets and stars, till finally it returns to the source of all creation.' Rushton's pleasant drawl remained, but there was a metallic ring behind it as if a machine was transmitting a programmed message.

'We were the first growth of that branch, my dear, but we degenerated. We disobeyed our master, turned away from our goal and mated with inferiors. Over the centuries our bodies became small and stunted and our former powers weakened till our neighbours ceased to fear us. Here on this sacred mountain they destroyed the flesh, but our true selves could not perish. It was decreed that the spirit should wander from one host to another till strength and devotion were reborn and we became reunited.' His old eyes strayed over the hillside and without physical proof Tania would have believed him insane. But the evidence was there to justify the statement: Ryder and Demchinsky sitting behind her in their ragged clothes and young men's bodies.

The Swine of Gadara – The Wandering Jew. Two stories merging into one, she had thought. For thirty centuries Daran's creatures had walked alone, moving from one human body to another, dreaming a dream they could never understand till one day Daniel Ryder discovered its significance and realized what he was. An avatar – a reincarnation – a Moses, whose mission was to gather his people together and take them home. So the notes of an aircraft had gone pulsing across the earth to imitate a chant that had once sounded over the crags of Allt y Cnicht, and the call was heard and answered.

The Land Rover had drawn up and some forty men and women had been waiting at the start of the climb. The rest of the archaeologists, Michael Turner, and other men and women Tania did not recognize. The would-be destroyers of her own race, but how Tania hoped she could help them!

'You might say that the occult and modern science have joined forces, Tania.' Ryder had leaned over her shoulder. 'My invention brought us together and Hans Graebe was the second architect. Without resistance built up over a long period, nobody can survive the demons created at Linsleat, but those children I brought to Treflys will survive. The drugs we provided them with contained a substance to defeat the coming epidemic.' He kept flexing his fingers as if proving they were his own. 'As has already happened with me, a transformation will take place. Our present bodies will perish with the rest of mankind, but our souls pass on to hosts that cannot be harmed.

'Yes, Tania, your people are going to be wiped out like dinosaurs, but if you do what we want . . . if you lead us to the spot Travers showed you, you and your husband may live. You will be given immunity and become joined with us before my aircraft release their cargoes to cleanse our world.'

'Live! As a parasite's host! With a monster lodged in my brain . . . destroying my personality.' Rushton was pulling her out of the car, the cord was biting into her flesh, but Tania swung round and spat in Ryder's face. 'I'd rather die a million times over.'

'Then so you shall. You'll die as slowly and painfully as Travers and Roberts died, and you are going to get a taste of what they suffered here and now.' Rushton's expression was still kindly, still friendly, but his eyes glinted almost as brightly as the cigarette-lighter that he took from his pocket. With Ryder holding her against the car door, he snapped on the flame and brought it up towards her face.

'Stop that. There is no need for brutality.' Hans Graebe stepped beside them. 'Lady Levin will be a good, sensible girl, because I came prepared for such an emergency.' Something else glinted and Tania felt a prick on her shoulder. What happened to our friend Demchinsky gave me the idea that more gentle persuasion might be required, and don't be impatient. This stuff works rather faster than Pentothal.

'Doesn't it, dear lady?' He bowed gallantly and replaced the syringe in his jacket. 'Are you ready to help us . . . to lead us to the exact spot Dr Travers showed you?'

'He didn't show me . . . he didn't actually point it out.' Tania felt physically faint, but all her terror and loathing had vanished. For some reason it was vitally important to win Graebe's approval, and she concentrated on recalling the way Travers's eye had kept moving from the map to the window. 'But though I'm not sure, I can't promise, but I do . . . do want to help . . . do want to take you there.'

She had done so. The goal was in sight and they were standing before a narrow opening in the cliffs that led up to the summit. Inside the fissure men were breaking through a wall and beyond that wall was something that held her companions spellbound. She looked at Graebe's face, which was set like a rigid metal mask, and laid her hands on his arm.

'What is it – please tell me what are you looking for – what you hope to find in there.'

'Hope? What do I hope for, meine gnädige Frau?' The English and German words were spoken slowly as though they were unfamiliar to him. 'Ich hoffe . . . hope for a miracle . . . that after drei tausend Jahre, mein . . .' He paused, and then resumed in a language Tania had never heard before.

*   *   *

At last the time was up. Willie Price looked at his watch and pulled the exploder towards him. The lights had vanished and he could carry out Missus's final order. He laid a hand on the magneto plunger, prepared to drive it home and then his arm stiffened. Another man was up on the ridge and Missus had told him to wait till they were all inside the mountain.

Nobody must escape, he had to kill them all. To lift the curse every single one of them had to die.

★   ★   ★

Somewhere beyond a crag called the Knight's Visor, Travers had said, and surely this was it? Mark had halted beneath a clump of boulders and he stared uncertainly around him. There were no lights to be seen, nothing moved at all and the cliffs ahead looked smooth and impregnable. The ridge leading towards them was very narrow, the northern side almost vertical, but gentler scree shoots fell away to his right.

Where the hell could they be? He hurried on in desperation because there was nothing else he could do. Less than five minutes ago he had seen the torches distinctly, but now Tania and her captors had vanished as if the earth or the sky had swallowed them.

The sky – a hostile sky that had sent one of its minions to mock him, to jeer at his failure and laugh at Tania's fate. He looked up, searching for the aircraft which was throbbing overhead, knowing that his sanity was going because he wanted to curse and shake his fist at a piece of machinery, and then he came to a stumbling halt. Apart from a few drifting clouds the sky was empty and the sound was not machine-made. It was more melodious, more rhythmic and tuneful than any Skyrider he had ever heard. What he was listening to was human voices. A chant full of threat and triumph that seemed to be coming from the cliffs, booming out along the ridge like a lighthouse siren to guide him. Hopelessness vanished, exhaustion fell away, and as if oxygen had been pumped into his lungs, adrenalin into his veins, Mark sprang forward.

Chapter Nineteen

'Ullah – rhalo – alla.' Though he was getting near to them, the voices were softer and the chant had lost its triumphant menace and sunk to a dirge, a mutter of awe and adoration, a cry of lost love. Lower and lower it sank and finally vanished as Mark started to edge his way into the cliff.

The place Mr Justice Roberts had found was a crack in the rocks that stank of rotting vegetation and was so narrow that Mark had to squeeze sideways against the lichen which covered the walls. But others had recently passed before him, and here and there the lichen had been rubbed away to reveal the carved symbols that Tania had seen in the exercise-book and the photograph from the safe. And not merely symbols: the tunnel was widening, his lighter flame lit up a chiselled slab and he gasped as a line of faces stared back at him.

Mark had half-expected to find pictures: battle and hunting scenes, depictions of human sacrifice; possibly ritual torture. But nothing like this, and, looking at the original appearance of Daran's people, he understood why they had been hated, why the massacre took place, why Roberts had considered them evil. They had been ill. They had flat faces, ravaged faces, faces with swollen, distorted features like carnival masks. 'Lion-faced' was a medical term for the condition. The old ones had been struck by an epidemic – maybe plague, perhaps leprosy – and the survivors had lived on with the poison in their veins ... immune warriors whose weapons were disease. Then, at some period the germ strain had lost its virulence or died and the Celts realized that their enemies could be conquered.

'Ullyo – ullya – ullam.' The chanting was resumed, lights

glowed ahead and Mark stepped over the remains of a broken wall. Tania was very close, but so were the creatures whose aim was destruction. The 'elden, sicken folke' were reunited to bring pestilence to the earth. Without any idea of what he could do when he reached them – his only hope was that Tania was unharmed – he walked on and then stopped in his tracks.

A cave opened out before him, and though lime deposits screened any traces of carvings, he sensed that it had once been used as a place of worship. Certainly that was the case now. Torches had been placed around the walls; in their light he could see a semicircle of kneeling figures and for a moment he joined them in a prayer of gratitude and love – because Tania was safe. She was standing to the right of the group and though her wrists were tied together and she looked dazed, she had not been injured. He started to creep slowly towards her, realizing that if a single one of those bowed heads was raised he would be seen.

'Ullah – ullalo – we are here.' Professor Rushton knelt in front of the others, between a young man Mark had noticed about the village and an elderly man with vivid auburn hair who he fancied must be Hans Graebe. 'All of us – ullaro ullan – all who heard the call have responded.' Partly in English and partly in the old language that had been imitated by an aircraft engine, Rushton's voice rang around the cave. Mark crept on and then halted, fighting back a cry of astonishment. The three leaders had stood up and he could see the thing before which they had been kneeling.

The legends all agreed that Daran could not die, but he looked dead enough. The Celts had buried him in one of his own temples and the fossilized body lay trapped beneath a granite slab. Even through the thick shell of limestone that had accumulated over the centuries it was possible to see how he had been killed. The broken limbs were unnaturally hinged, there was a depression in the skull, and rocks had flattened the rib-cage. The whole figure was vast, much much bigger than any human being, and either Daran had been a giant or the lime deposits had multiplied his size three times over. If the first possibility was correct, the cavern must once have had another entrance that had been blocked deliberately or closed by a landslide.

'Free him.' Rushton raised his hand and four men stood up and left the semicircle. They worked with extreme reverence and returned to their knees when the slab had been removed from the huge stone body.

'Ul – loulla – lo. Wake, master. Return to us, Daran.' The young man beside Rushton was speaking, but it was Daniel Ryder's voice Mark heard and its passion told him that time was running out. He had to reach Tania quickly because the creatures were not merely evil – soon they would be berserk.

Mark had accepted reincarnation as a fact because the evidence was there before him. He had to accept that one soul could enter and possess another's body; Rushton's voice proved that. He had begun to believe that Daran and his people might be true aliens – invaders from another planet who had degenerated in terrestrial conditions. But he did not for one moment credit the possibility that physical life could exist without heat or light or nourishment.

But Daran's people did, and the belief might destroy Tania. They really believed that a heart still functioned beneath the thick coating of rock and that their master's shattered body would answer their call.

'Hear us, Great One.' Hans Graebe had turned and stooped beside the figure, and Mark saw tears pouring from his eyes. Those pitiless eyes that had once viewed experiments to produce disease in human beings . . . that had watched the growth of *Genus Linsleatensis* with professional satisfaction.

'Must I help you then, Daran?' Graebe lifted a hammer very gently. Soon the delusion would be apparent to them; the limestone would break away and all they would find would be the dust of a mortal being who died on the day the Celts entombed him. When that happened, disappointment and anguish might blaze into violence and Tania reap the results.

'Ullya – aranul – Meister.' Graebe was chipping at the monstrous forehead and a fragment of limestone flaked off. Apart from his voice and the tap of the hammer, the cave was in complete silence, but tension flowed from all of them like a gas being compressed into a solid. At any moment Daran's death would be proved a fact and there was no time left. Mark braced himself to spring towards Tania and then felt something jerk in his pocket: the tape-recorder which had a protective rubber covering, and there was just a chance that its mechanism might withstand the shock. He pressed a switch and hurled it forward. The ruse worked.

'Ullah – zu-zu-zah – zazullah.' The recorder had fallen in shadow, and, as the aircraft exhausts rang out, the chanting resumed, and it was full of joy and triumph again. Daran's people were shuffling forward on their knees, they were craning over him waiting for the rock to split open, waiting to see his face. A miracle had been achieved and the resurrection accomplished. Their master's actual flesh had conquered death, and it was his voice that was calling to them.

'Ullah – azah – zullah.' Voices and mechanism had joined together, roaring and booming around the walls of the cave, and Mark had rejoined Tania. He had his hand on her arm, he was pulling her round, he was dragging her to safety, but why didn't she respond? Why did she resist and fight against him and keep twisting her body towards the left? His own body stiffened with nausea as he saw the horror in her eyes. Was he too late? Had an alien intelligence been planted in her brain already?

'No, darling ... wait ... must wait ... must look at – ' She screamed aloud and Mark followed her stare, because another sound had been added to the voices and the tape-recording, and he saw a sight which would haunt him till his dying day.

The limestone was flaking away of its own accord, and behind it something that looked like living tissue was moving ... something that looked like a pair of open lips.

And then they were running. He had torn his eyes away from the sight, he had slapped Tania hard across the face and at last she was obeying him. They were stumbling through the cave, with the chant of triumph rising in crescendo. They were past the broken wall and squeezing along the fissure. They were out into the open air, seeing the stars overhead, and their feet were pounding across rock and heather. They were running to freedom, but nobody bothered to stop them, because a god had defeated the grave – a sleeping giant had awakened.

They were free, they were safe, the scree shoots were falling away to the south and the lights of the village were gleaming to welcome them. They were almost halfway along the ridge when the voice of Allt y Cnicht joined the voice of Daran.

Willie Price had exploded the dynamite, the mountain shuddered, the earth reared up and swept them forward.

Postscript

MAN-MADE AVALANCHE – TRAGIC DEATH-ROLL – MIRACULOUS ESCAPE OF NOBEL PRIZE-WINNER AND WIFE – THE HORROR OF ALLT Y CNICHT. A man sat in a waiting-room, killing time with a selection of newspapers. To avoid any general panic – because the being called Daran had survived rocks before, and Graebe's germ culture had been buried with him – it was a very diluted version of the story that had been issued to the press.

When Kirk had arrived at Treflys, and Mark and Tania were strong enough to tell him what they had experienced, the general had immediately sworn Bragshaw to secrecy and dictated a statement in their joint names.

Willie Price was Kirk's sole scapegoat, and everybody else an innocent victim. Willie had been engulfed with all the others by the landslide he created, and it was unlikely that any of the bodies would be recovered; most unlikely. Tania had been shown that lethal fountain-pen in Graebe's pocket and, unknown to the public, Kirk had arranged that no recovery attempts would be made.

But Willie's bicycle and fingerprints had been found at the dynamite store and it was clear what had happened. Willie had killed Megan Ryder in a fit of madness and gone rushing to Dr Travers for help and absolution. Then, when the doctor had tried to telephone the police, Willie's mania had flared up again and he had tortured the old man to death and decided to end his own life dramatically.

The fate of the archaeologists was a most tragic coincidence. They and a number of companions, which included Dr Hans Graebe, the distinguished German chemist, two young visitors to Treflys, and possibly other persons not yet identified, had been exploring a cave when the explosion occurred and they must have died instantaneously. But fate had been kinder to Sir Marcus and Lady Levin, out walking by moonlight. By lucky chance a scree shoot had carried them down the easier southern slopes and they had escaped with concussion and minor injuries.

'Where – just where have I seen that hill before?' The man was looking at two photographs in the *Daily Globe*. Before the explosion Allt y Cnicht had been an imposing mountain, but now most of the summit had vanished and it had a mean and stunted appearance. What is it about the place that disturbs me? he asked himself, studying the earlier shot. He had never been to Wales, and to the best of his knowledge these were the only pictures of Allt y Cnicht he had ever seen, but the first one appeared uncannily familiar.

'Oh dear! That could knock the shares if there's anything seriously wrong.' The man had money invested in Rydercraft Aviation and he frowned at an announcement that all their planes were to be called in for engine modifications. But though he might suffer financial loss it was the photographs that still held his interest. Why was he reminded of that mountain? Where had he seen it before? *Déjà vu*, perhaps. He had a keen personal interest in psychology and the phenomenon might provide a solution.

'Mr Smith – Mr Smith?' The receptionist had to raise her voice before the man looked up. Six months ago a virus infection had damaged his eardrums and he was very deaf. Even loud noises escaped him when he was not wearing his hearing aid. 'Will you come through, sir?'

'Of course.' He screwed in the aid and followed her to another room. A very restful and dimly lit room with a decor designed to soothe its visitors.

'Ah, there you are, Mr Smith. Nice to see you.' Like the room, its owner had a soothing manner. He shook his guest's hand, inquired about his journey and waved him into an arm-chair.

'First, let's see what your own medical adviser has to say about you, Mr Smith.' He moved behind his desk and unfolded a letter. 'Ah, the trouble started shortly *before* your hearing was impaired? Might be a connection, I shouldn't wonder. So much physical illness stems from up here.' He tapped his forehead. 'When the first incident occurred, you were on a flight to Paris. Had a mental blackout and became violent when the air hostess restrained you. Fined twenty-five pounds; tch, tch. And, though there's been nothing like that again, some after-effects persist.

'However, helpful as these notes are, we'll forget them for the moment. To get a good first impression of your problem, I must have it in your own words – from the horse's mouth, as they say.' He laid down the letter with a man-to-man smile to put his visitor at ease. 'Speak quite freely and don't let anything embarrass you. I am as dispassionate as a priest in the confessional and my only interest is to help you.'

'And how I hope that you can help me.' The man had turned his hearing aid towards the desk, but he couldn't concentrate because his thoughts kept returning to Allt y Cnicht. Where – just where had he seen that mountain before? On a calendar, or a postcard, or a travel film? The explanation must be quite simple, but every contour of the hill seemed so completely familiar, as clear to him as his own garden. 'Dr Mason will have told you I have been sleeping badly, and the pills he prescribed have not helped me at all.'

While he spoke he pictured the long ridges leading up to the summit, the plunging cliffs on one side and the scree shoots to the south. 'For the last six months I have been troubled by a recurring dream – a nightmare that never varies in a single detail.'

Printed in Great Britain
by Amazon

4192S845R00108